Gloria & Ron's
Best of
Wishes,
Always!
Ken

KENNETH BARTHOLOMEW A NOVEL

SENTENCED

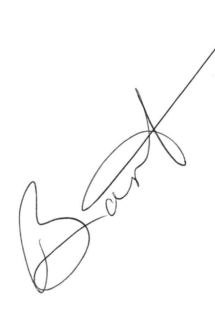

SENTENCED

ISBN 978-1-66787-289-6 (Print)
ISBN 978-1-66787-290-2 (eBook)

DEDICATION

FOR TWYLA, my beautiful and brilliant wife and proofreader. Thank you for your patience, your insight, and your unerring advice.

PROLOGUE

T HE SLENDER NEEDLE SLID BENEATH THE SKIN OF THE EXTERNAL ear canal, penetrating the lowest space of the middle ear compartment and finding the jugular bulb, which relays blood from the brain directly to the heart. He pushed the plunger on the syringe, flooding the blood stream with the concentrated solution of potassium chloride. On arrival at its destination, the potassium instantly paralyzed the heart muscles. All activity ceased.

Perfectly motionless, ever patient, he waited for the blood pressure to drop to zero and the blood to congeal slightly, avoiding telltale back bleeding when he removed the needle. Satisfied, he took the extra precaution of using his otoscope to mash a sticky lump of earwax over the needle site, knowing that, in an autopsy, they would pay scant attention to the ear canal once they ascertained no trauma, no blood behind the eardrum.

The cleaning lady would find the body Monday morning, along with the alcohol and cocaine used to sedate the mark, and the authorities would write it off as another cocaine heart attack. *No matter,* he thought as he packed up his instruments, *by that time, I'll be safely on a beach hundreds of miles from here, my alibi airtight.*

1

"WHO EXACTLY HAS THE RIGHT TO KILL? I DON'T KNOW HOW you can say that without flinching." The voice echoed through the doorway as Dr. Bryce Thompson strode into the doctors' lounge for a cup of coffee that cold Monday morning. The spring Montana sun was trying vainly to warm the thin mountain air as it peeked red and golden over the snowcapped ridge to the east.

"Oh, good lord! Are you two at it again?" he said as he stepped to the Keurig and brewed a strong cup of Columbian.

Ray Littleton, brilliant general surgeon, and Antonio Malandra, equally brilliant pathologist, were having their customary morning tête-à-tête over coffee and protein bars while they awaited setup in Operating Room #3.

"Ray thinks we should just kill people and that would end murder," Dr. Malandra retorted, smiling at his own wit. "He forgets that two negatives only make a positive in mathematics."

"And Doctor Holier-Than-Thou thinks we should forgive and forget and spend millions housing sociopathic animals incapable of rehabilitation," Littleton countered. "I'm just stating the obvious.

Most of the guys on death row are damaged goods. Overall, society would be healthier if you cut them out, just like a person is healthier if you amputate the gangrenous leg or cut out the tumor before it kills the host."

"What say you, Doctor Thompson? You don't frequent our lounge long enough to share your thoughts on such weighty matters," Malandra asked.

"Yes. Chime in here, Bryce. You spend all day trying to improve the lives of sick and dying patients, spending tens of thousands of dollars to prolong a ninety-year-old woman's life by six months, maybe a year. Your patients have contributed to society and now need the resources that the mongrels on death row are using up. Wouldn't you like some of those resources for Grandma Smith so she can spend a few more years seeing her grandkids?"

Bryce took an airy sip of coffee, trying not to burn his lips. Stalling, his hazel-green eyes scrutinized the two doctors in the worn-leather lounge chairs, his six-foot-four frame filling the doorway as he edged to make his escape. "I guess I would have to side with Tony on this one, Ray. I realize that oaths don't mean much these days in a society where it's take what you can get while you can get it, but we all took an oath to protect life. I'll leave the taking of life to others, thank you very much."

"Hah!" Malandra grinned, pointing at Littleton. "Two to one. You lose."

"Not so fast," Littleton retorted, gesturing toward Bryce. "What if you were faced with an inescapable predicament? A predicament where you had to make a decision. One where you couldn't wait and let someone else take the responsibility. Take this scenario. Your wife is being raped by a gang of four, and you have a gun. Do you let them finish or do you shoot?"

"Well, that's a bit theoretical, isn't it?"

"It's all theoretical, for Christ's sake. Would you shoot or let them have their way?"

"Come on, Ray. That would be more of a self-defense question than a cold-blooded murder question. A guy on death row is imprisoned and incapable of hurting anyone at that point. How do you justify taking the life of a defenseless person?" Bryce took another sip of coffee and sidestepped closer toward the door.

"Don't answer a question with a question. Do you shoot, or do you let them have their way because you don't believe in killing? And you better know, the minute they see you holding a gun, they are gonna start shooting."

"Again, that is a self-defense question. Just as in war, protecting your life or the life of others is not considered murder."

"So, you agree. It is okay to take a life."

"I guess I would shoot to wound, not to kill."

"Oh, be real. You're a seasoned hunter and a damn good shot with a rifle, but you know as well as anyone that rapid-fire shooting with a pistol is a different game entirely. You shoot to kill, or you die. And the hit rate is so low, you better hope you have a beefy sixteen-round clip and not a lightweight revolver."

"There you bring in intent, again, Ray. If I intend to wound but end up killing to save myself or another, that is entirely different than cold-blooded killing."

"It's still killing. We were asking if it is okay to take a life, and you just justified it."

"I wouldn't say justified. I would say rationalized."

"Semantics. They're still dead." Littleton turned and pointed at Malandra. "You lose."

"Well, I would just love to stay and quibble, but Grandma Smith's electrolytes need adjusting, and her heart failure needs my help. I actually have to work to make money. We poor family docs can't make a million a year slicing and dicing failing body parts." Bryce turned on his heel and headed for the medical ward. Grandma Smith's potassium was 5.5, and her kidney function was waning. *Yes, she is going to die,* he pondered as he walked toward the ICU, *but not today. Not on my watch. Not if I can help it.*

2

MORNING ROUNDS TOOK LONGER THAN EXPECTED, AS USUAL, and Bryce was feeling the time crunch as he walked to the clinic, knowing he would probably be late for his first patient, as usual. Entering by the back entrance where impatient patients and overzealous drug reps couldn't sidetrack him, he was met by Maryann, Bev, and Lynelle, three of the smartest and hardest working nurses he had the good fortune to have on his team.

"Mrs. Swanson is having palpitations, and we haven't checked electrolytes lately. Can I have a verbal for a BMP?" Maryann inquired as she sought approval to order a Basic Metabolic Panel.

"Better make it a Complete Metabolic Panel. She likes her martinis and her liver's been working overtime."

Bev handed Bryce a pile of mail. "Mr. Crawford is retaining fluid and says his legs feel like logs. Can we bump his Lasix? He's already on 80 BID."

"Is he here?" Bryce asked as he slid behind his desk and began logging in on his desktop.

"No. Phone call."

"Get him in here. We need to check his potassium, but he also has hypothyroidism. We need a TSH and a Renal Panel."

Lynelle jumped in with her question almost before Bryce finished that last one. "Bill Bradford came early for his eleven o'clock and insists on being seen right away. He needs to leave town, and his pressure is 178 over 90."

"Just bring him back to my office. We're titrating his blood pressure meds and that should only take a minute—unless he's having other problems?"

"Nothing mentioned."

"OK, bring him back," Bryce said as he finished logging in and cued his lab inbox. Staring back at him, Bryce saw a critically high creatinine level on his ICU patient and called back to the hospital with new orders. "Just another day in paradise," he mumbled as he shed his jacket and took a sip of the steaming coffee Bev always had ready for him. He didn't think twice about the multitasking; it becomes a way of life for doctors, and those who can't handle the staccato pace don't gravitate to primary care.

By noon, he was pretty much back on schedule when his secretary buzzed him. "Your brother, Detective Thompson, is here and wants to talk to you. He bribed us with a large supreme and a medium Canadian bacon and pineapple. Can I send him back?"

"Sure. At least we're getting lunch today." Bryce seldom left his desk for lunch unless it was to run across the street to the hospital for an emerging problem. Pizza sounded better than a granola bar.

"Hey, little brother," Bill Thompson said as the burly, ex-tight end balanced two paper plates loaded with pizza, kicked the door shut with one foot, and slid one of the paper plates across Bryce's desk as he slumped into a chair, his ever-serious demeanor more serious than usual. "We have another body," he said as he took a huge bite of supreme. "It looks like a cocaine heart attack, but there's a twist. By the way, thanks for doing that medical record review for me on Corsello. I'm a bit confused and need to talk with you about that one sometime, when we aren't so rushed. Okay?"

"Of course. So, what's this latest one?"

"Zebrowski, William, 56, Caucasian, wealthy businessman. Liked his happy hour but not known to use drugs. Found dead in his home office with cocaine and paraphernalia on the desk. He was dead for a day or two. Wife was out of town. Cleaning lady found him early last Monday morning. Coroner is calling it presumptive cocaine heart attack. Final autopsy reports pending. Prelim confirms cocaine in the bloodstream."

"So, what do you need from me? Sounds pretty cut-and-dried."

"I know, but something doesn't seem right on this one. It's been bugging me all week, and I wanted to refresh my thinking. Tell me about cocaine heart attacks. How common are they?"

"Fairly common. Even young people have them. Remember that college basketball player years ago, Len Bias? He was a first round NBA draft pick but dropped dead from snorting cocaine. It's a classic teaching case because it demonstrates the cardiotoxicity of the drug. He had no other drugs in his system. His heart was big and strong, and no structural abnormalities were found at autopsy.

"Cocaine is a stimulant. That's why some users feel like they are so on top of things, so energized, so indestructible, until they crash. However, it can also overstimulate the heart in certain people, and it's impossible to predict who will be sensitive and who won't. When the heart gets that stimulated, it can go out of its normal rhythm into a very fast rhythm, and that makes it very, very inefficient at pumping blood. When that happens, they can suffer irreversible brain and heart damage in only four or five minutes from lack of oxygen delivery. Then the heart slows and stops completely. They call it a cocaine heart attack in common jargon, but it's really a cocaine-induced arrhythmia that kills them, not a blocked artery like a typical heart attack."

"And arrhythmia in plain English means abnormal rhythm?"

"Precisely."

"And how much does it take? Cocaine, I mean."

"Very little in the right person. Some people have high tolerance, and some are supersensitive, and like I said, you can't predict which group any one person belongs to. Maybe we can group them as we learn more from genetic analysis, but not using is the only safe route."

Bryce had barely started on his pizza as he watched Bill bolt down his fourth piece, throw the plate in the trash, and walk to the large corner windows of Bryce's office. He was staring out across the greening Helena Valley, but he wasn't enjoying the spring thaw. Bryce knew that look; he had known it all his life. Bill was lost in thought, looking but not seeing. He might as well be in the void between the mountains bordering their valley.

"Something just smells wrong with this one," Bill said, his gaze still focused on the infinity beyond Sleeping Giant Mountain to the north. "I have interviewed everybody I could find who knew Zebrowski, and not a single person as much as implied that he used coke. So, assuming it's his first time, he doesn't know his limits, takes too much, and wakes up dead. I'll buy that, but wouldn't a first-time user just experiment a little? Maybe take a little hit off a fingernail or a tiny snort?"

"You would think so, but drug users don't exactly follow logic when it comes to getting high. Don't confuse a rational person's motives and behaviors with someone who has a mental illness or an addiction."

"I get that, but this guy had three lines neatly razored out and a bunch in his system. It's just been bugging me all week. I even went back to the evidence lab and confirmed something that was bothering me. There were no fingerprints on the razor. I don't know, it's probably nothing, but my cop's sixth sense keeps drawing it up to the surface, like a piece of driftwood that won't sink."

"When did you ever let anything not bother you until you had it neatly wrapped and labeled and on a shelf somewhere, either in an evidence locker or in that weirdly wired brain of yours?"

"Oh, look who's talking," Bill laughed. He turned back into the room and just as quickly he was back in the present. "Any thoughts?"

"I agree, if, and I do mean if, he was a first timer. But there are countless stories of people hiding it from their loved ones for years until their lives slowly come off the rails. You mentioned a wife. What does she have to say about it?"

"She's been studying art in Paris. It was hard to locate her. She just flew in yesterday but swears she knew nothing about cocaine use. Acted just as shocked as anyone. Seemed dumbfounded to me, just ashen-faced and blank, like a half-lit neon sign saying 'no one's home.'"

"Well, her life just got turned upside down. She just lost her life mate, and things will never be the same for her again. Not that you would understand. You won't ever let a woman get that close."

"Hey! No lectures right now, professor. But you are right. Things will never be the same for her again because she now has his bank accounts and the business equity, plus the five-million-dollar life insurance policy she took out on him recently. Oh, no. Things will never be the same for her again."

"Maybe you should get close to her."

"Funny man today, aren't you?"

"Hey, I better catch up with some charting. Anything else?"

"No, that cocaine stuff was pretty much as I remembered it. I just wanted to refresh my memory. I'll get out of your hair, but when can we go over that Corsello case?"

"I promised Nicole I would help her tonight. How about tomorrow evening? You can come over and help me move some heavy timbers into the back yard, and we can talk."

"Perfect. Thanks. I owe ya."

The afternoon went largely as the morning had gone, walk-ins crowding the schedule, taking time away from patients already scheduled for weeks, and Bryce was tired when he left for home that evening. Nicole was waiting for him with a glass of sauvignon blanc, and he could smell the garlic bread when he walked in from the garage. "Ooh. Smells wonderful in here. What's cooking?" he asked as he kissed her and took his glass of wine.

"Pheasant Marsala in cream sauce with mushrooms and scallions over wild rice," she answered as they clinked glasses. "Cheers!"

The fact that Nicole had her own glass of wine did not go unnoticed. "Negative again?"

Her shoulders slumped under her long blond hair, and Bryce immediately regretted broaching the subject as a tear began to well against the baby blue. "I guess I'm just not supposed to be a mother," she said as she blinked it away. "It's certainly not for lack of trying," Nicole added, trying to sound upbeat. "It's just not fair. High school girls get pregnant every ten minutes, and I can't snag one stray sperm. And based on the tests, I know you aren't the problem, so it must be me."

"It'll happen, Hon. Sooner or later, it'll happen." He pulled her close and kissed her gently. "Remember your cousin's story. The minute they adopted, her nesting hormones kicked in after seven years, and she got pregnant within a month of the adoption. Two babies ten months apart. It's not uncommon."

"Not common enough for me," she answered as she plated the steaming garlic bread. "And I'll take sooner rather than later, thank you very much," she added as they walked into the four-season porch, the beautiful Montana valley unfolding below them under the golden glow of the sun settling behind the snowcapped Bitterroots to the west.

"Bill came by today," Bryce said between bites of garlic bread as they settled into their wicker couch.

"What's Bill been up to?"

"He's investigating another death, and it's bugging him. You know Bill. If everything isn't perfect, if there's some little thing he can't figure out, he can't let it go."

"Gee, who does that remind me of?" Nicole laughed, poking him in the ribs.

"Stop it. You're going to make me spill," he squirmed, twisting away from her probing fingers. "Anyway, he's going to come over tomorrow after work to discuss another case, the one I reviewed the medical records on two weeks ago."

"What about my project? You promised me those raised garden beds with the folding greenhouse covers."

"That's why I invited him over. He's going to help me move all that lumber into position. It'll save me a bunch of time, not to mention my back, and we can talk while we work."

"I better cook up something special."

"No, let's just have sandwiches out on the deck so we can keep working and get a lot done before dark."

"Sounds good. I'm excited. With those folding covers, I can get an early garden in this spring. And hopefully, by fall, I'll have a belly this big and won't have to bend over so far," she added as she swept her arms around an imaginary tummy. "In fact," she added as she snuggled against him and took his wine glass out of his hand, "I think supper can wait a little bit longer." She kissed him hard on the lips as she pulled him down onto the couch.

"Or give the dose herself."

"No. She was out of town that night. Airtight alibi. She has credit card receipts, hotel bills, and room service charges with her signature on them."

They shared sandwiches and thoughts for several more minutes and Bill was preparing to leave when Nicole stepped out onto the deck. "Cold sandwiches are poor wages for the work you did tonight, Sir William. How about Friday night for lasagna and a fine bottle of wine?"

"Your lasagna? Wild horses couldn't keep me away. What time? And what can I bring?"

"How about seven? You just bring your appetite, and I'll try my best to satisfy it."

"Awesome. See you then."

Bill finished his beer and left for home. "That was nice, Nic," Bryce said as Bill disappeared around the corner, "to invite him over for Friday."

"Well, I can invite a party of six, or I can invite Bill. The amount of food is still the same," she laughed.

"He sure made my life easier by getting this all done tonight. Now I can work on the folding covers."

"Ooh, I'm excited to finally have a garden again. You go shower while I clean up this mess."

4

B Y FRIDAY EVENING, BRYCE HAD THE BASIC FRAMES BUILT FOR Nicole's project, and she was in high spirits as she put the finishing touches on their dinner. Bill came in through the garage, as per his usual, and kicked off his shoes as he hollered "Anyone home?" He closed the door and inhaled deeply. "Oh my God. It smells better than Caffè Molise in here. And I know it's going to taste better," he added as he sauntered into the kitchen and gave Nicole a hug as Bryce walked in from the great room. "I don't know what my lowlife brother ever did to deserve you, but I sure wish you had a sister."

Nicole picked up two glasses of pinot grigio and handed one to each of the men, then picked up a glass of water and toasted them. "Salute. You boys go take a seat. Caprese salads are on the table. I'll be right there."

They sat and enjoyed the meal as only family can. Bill was finishing his third helping when he turned to Nicole. "You know, Nic, I can never order lasagna in a restaurant anymore. You've spoiled me. Those acidic tomato sauces can't hold a candle to your creamy cheese sauce. If I knew how to cook anything other than hot dogs and hamburgers, I'd steal your recipe."

"It's yours when you want it. I'll even help you make it the first twenty or thirty times until you get it right," she laughed.

"No can do. If it doesn't start with hamburger and end with helper, it's out of my league."

She poured them another glass of wine and then started clearing the table. "You guys just relax. You've earned it this week," she said as she took an armful of dishes to the kitchen.

Bill took a sip and turned to Bryce. "You are never going to believe what came down yesterday. Talk about timing."

"What's that?"

"The insurance companies have been taking a bath in this region the past few years on life insurance. I know one of their VPs, and he wants me to look into it in my free time. But I need a huge favor, Bryce."

"Name it."

"There had been six deaths in this area in the past eight years with multimillion-dollar payouts. Corsello was number seven. That cocaine heart attack last week was number eight, and it's going to cost them another five million. The insurance companies compare notes, cross-checking for fraud and such. There's a huge spike in their actuarial tables for this area, significantly out of proportion to expected or historical numbers. With this much money on the line, they're looking for anything out of the ordinary."

"Interesting."

"But that's only the outer layer of this onion. He said if I can find any kind of fraud in any of these cases, which could save them millions, I'd be offered a full-time job as one of their chief investigators. It'll pay twice what I'm making with the PD, Bryce. Regular hours, sane schedules, twice the vacation days, paid seminars at destination locations. No more bagging street scum and drug dealers at 2 a.m., never knowing which one is going to open fire and end the dream. I love my job, but I'll admit it's getting old, and this sounds like heaven after all these years. Hell, I had fifteen years in with the force by the time you finished med school and residency. Come June, I'll have my twenty-year pin, and I can take early retirement from the force and double my income."

"OK. So where do I come in?"

"All of these deaths look like plain old bad luck. No red flags anywhere. No trauma except one motorcycle accident. No toxicology surprises. Nothing. But there's just been too many of them with these huge life insurance policies. Now, we both know numbers can deceive, but there is another twist. That Zebrowski case—the cocaine heart attack guy—turns out he was screwing a twenty-something secretary, and the wife found out. She has been traveling more than she has been at home, staying away from the guy, avoiding his calls, flying Delta One to London and Paris to pursue her art. According to one of her friends, she wanted nothing more than to get out. What's job one?"

"Establish motive."

"Bingo."

"And my job?"

"You know medicine, and I don't. Can I impose on you to look through their medical records, go over them with a fine-toothed comb and see if there is something, anything, that doesn't look right? I don't know what to look for. It could be staring me in the face, and I wouldn't recognize it, like that C-peptide-insulin-whatever-pro-whatever-whatever. I might as well be reading hieroglyphics."

"Do you have a deadline? I'm swamped, as usual. And I have to get Nicole's project done."

"No actual deadline. Just sooner than later. I don't know how long this job offer is on the table. It could get filled if I wait too long. And who knows? Maybe it's a dead end anyway. But I want to give it my best shot. Or should I say our best shot? I can't do it without you, Bro."

"OK. But we have HIPAA rules about looking into charts that we don't have reason or authorization to go into. I would need some type of clearance."

"I've got that covered. I've asked the insurance people to make duplicates of all their medical records. Everything. I'll have stacks and stacks of stuff. There are still some toxicologies pending on that latest autopsy, and I'll get you printouts when that's done. You can do this in the comfort of your own home with your trusty red pen. There will be no computer trails for you to worry about. Besides, I don't want anyone to know we're digging around. You know my suspicious little mind. I trust no one. I like to work quietly and not tip my hand."

"I'll try to help, but it sounds like a long shot. Don't get your hopes up."

"Thanks. I'll drop off the file boxes in the morning."

Nicole called from the kitchen doorway. "Dessert, anyone?"

"God, no," Bill said with an exaggerated moan as he rubbed his belly. "I'm ready to burst. I think I'll finish this wine and call my Uber driver. I need a good night's sleep but thank you."

They finished up, and in minutes, Bill's ride was there. They bid him good night, then Nicole turned to Bryce. "I could only hear bits and pieces of that. What's Bill got going?"

"He has some medical records he wants me to review. It looks like eight cases, so I can only hope they don't have huge records. Remember how long it took just to do that one for the state quality review board?"

"Oh, God! Do I. You went over every line, every tiny little entry. Doctor O.C.D. at his finest," she laughed. "But what can you do?"

"It's a long shot, but there've been seven high-dollar insurance payouts in the last few years, and last week's death makes number eight. Bill's being offered the carrot of a better job if he finds a link that will save the insurance companies big bucks. If I can find any kind of fraud in these cases, the job could be his."

"I guess I don't understand. What fraud?"

"Well, say a guy finds out he has a heart condition, so he takes out a five-million-dollar policy but hides or falsifies information. That's fraud, and they don't have to pay because he was sold a certain policy at a certain rate under false pretenses. If I find even one of them was fraudulent, they save millions, and Bill gets his dream job. He's tired of the grind on the force, and I don't blame him. He's worked his way up to lead detective from a high school education and night school. No one deserves it any more than he does."

"I agree. But if you do all the work, why don't you get paid for your time?"

"If they hired me directly, Bill wouldn't get the credit. Besides, they have doctors on their payroll, and they haven't found anything. They want a detective to do what detectives do. Like if there's foul play but no one is picking up on it."

"It still looks like you're doing it for free."

"I don't mind, Nic. Not in the least. You didn't know us back then. After Mom and Dad were killed by that drunk driver, Bill worked day and night to pay the bills and put food on the table so I could finish high school. Christ, I was only thirteen, and he was just finishing high school. He could have gone to college on a football scholarship, he was that good, but he gave up college and whatever other dreams he had so we could live in a fifty-foot trailer that had an old propane stove with two burners that didn't light and a heater that barely worked. He's one of the smartest men I know. He could have done anything. Instead, he raised me. I will never be able to pay him back. Never."

"You're right. I'm sorry. I was only thinking in the present. So, when do you start?"

"He'll drop off the files at the house tomorrow. He doesn't want to bring them to the clinic because he doesn't want anyone to know we're even working on this. Mums the word."

"I should be home all day. I'll put them in your office if he comes by while you're making rounds, but you have to promise me one thing."

"What's that?"

"You have to promise me you won't become obsessed and devote all your time to this."

"When have I ever become obsessed with something?"

"Oh, only when you're breathing and there's the slightest hint that there's a T that's not crossed."

"Okay, I promise. By the way, did I tell you that Hanson Trucking will be dropping off the black dirt in the morning? Have them dump it just to the east of the driveway, then I'll wheelbarrow it back to the gardens. After hospital rounds, I'm picking up the last of the PVC pipe and couplers. I'll need your help stretching and attaching the plastic, but I should have things ready for you to start planting by Sunday night."

"Ooh, you're the greatest. With frost and rabbit protection, I'll have fresh tomatoes way sooner than last year. Thanks, Hon," she said as she kissed him and held him tight. "I never want to let go."

5

FOUR WEEKS LATER FOUND BRYCE CARRYING A STEAMING CUP OF decaf coffee with extra French vanilla to Nicole's bedside. He had always been an early riser, and this day was no different. She squinted awake at the early spring sun peeking into their master bedroom.

"I've got to get going," he said as he bent to kiss her. "I've got a sickie in the ICU, a full morning at the clinic, and some pathology questions for Doctor Malandra."

"Ooh, thanks, Hon," she cooed as she blew across the steaming surface and took a tentative sip. "Have you looked at the gardens recently? I already have green shoots." She took another sip. "Thanks for the coffee. I don't know how you get by on so little sleep, but I sure love it."

"Love you. See you this afternoon."

He kissed her again and headed for the hospital. Morning rounds went like clockwork, and he walked down to the pathology department to find Tony Malandra. He strolled into the inner sanctums of the department and was greeted by the toothy smile of the teaching skeleton wired together anatomically and hanging from a roller stand. Two medical students were examining the bones.

"Good morning, gentlemen."

"Good morning, Doctor Thompson. Can you show us where the rotator cuff originates? Jack says it's here, and I say it's here," the taller one said, pointing to the top of the scapula.

"Well, you're both right, and you're both wrong," he said as he walked up to 'Eve,' as she was affectionately called by the medical students. "Just remember the acronym SITS. The four muscles that contribute to the rotator cuff tendons are the supraspinatus, infraspinatus, teres minor, and subscapularis, here, here, here, and here," he explained as he pointed to the four depressions on the shoulder blade where the muscles attached. "Remember, the SITS muscles "sit" on the scapula, and you can bet it will be on your board exams."

"Oh, now I remember that from gross anatomy. It's cool to have this skeleton right here."

"Yes, Doctor Malandra is very resourceful," Bryce added.

"Thanks, Doctor Thompson," they called as he walked on through the lab.

"Morning, Bryce," Tony Malandra said without looking up from where he was examining tissue slides under the microscope. "To what do we owe the pleasure of your visit to the bowels of Valhalla? Did your Valkyries get lost?"

"Must have, because none of my patients end up down here," he retorted.

"What's up? Did you get a questionable path report?"

"Sort of. I'm on the state quality assurance board, and I was doing a death review and had a couple of questions. I know you contract with the county for a lot of our autopsies since they are so shorthanded in Missoula. You did the one on a fifty-six-year-old male named William Zebrowski. The housekeeper found him in his home on a Monday morning, presumably after a weekend of partying. The wife was out of town. He was found with cocaine and alcohol in his system, but I noticed there was little other reporting of body fluids. Isn't it standard to do vitreous humor levels on things like electrolytes, potassium leaching curves for time of death, glucose, and presence or absence of drugs?"

"Yeah, we mostly do electrolytes, alcohol, and sometimes toxicology on vitreous, depending on the circumstances, but on that case, he was seen that weekend by his housekeeper and was found early Monday morning by the housekeeper. There was no sign of trauma. The body temperature degradation curve was consistent with that time frame, so time of death was never a question. Plus, time of death as determined by the potassium leaching curve is seldom used anymore, so there was no need. It's kind of a judgment call."

"But what about drug levels if there was a poisoning?"

"He had a high blood alcohol level and a high cocaine level and nothing else. Pretty open-and-shut. These are cocaine arrhythmia deaths. We see it all the time."

"No, I understand that, but the wife stands to get a check for five million. What if he was poisoned? The vitreous is isolated from the rest of the body by the protective layers of the eye, making it a separate compartment and slower to change than most bodily fluids. If someone used a drug on a routine basis, you would find it in the vitreous because it would have had time to equilibrate there, right? But if they were poisoned, there would be cocaine in the blood, as found in this case, but little or none would have had time to accumulate in the vitreous, so there would be a mismatch. That's where my reading is taking me. Am I thinking about this right?"

"I guess you're technically correct, Bryce, but we have to make judgment calls down here just like you have to make them up on the wards. You can't run every test on every patient every day, or you would bankrupt the system. We have the same constraints down here. The county must pick up the bill on most of these autopsies, and they have a budget. We are happy to contract for them at a discount, but we have a bottom line too."

"When you get one of these autopsy requests, do you get much background? Social or medical history? Or are they all just cold, hard, technical stuff?"

"One of our most common would be a homeless bum found in a shack or under a bridge, no social history and no medical records. Or a gunshot or knife fight, your typical Saturday night special. Maybe some medical records but usually not much."

"Anything on this particular guy?"

"Nothing I can remember as out of the ordinary."

"OK. Thanks Tony."

Bryce turned and ambled past the medical students still examining Eve as he left the department.

6

FIVE WEEKS LATER, BRYCE'S SECRETARY INTERRUPTED HIS REVerie. "Doctor Thompson, your brother is here, bribing us with fresh donuts. Can I bring him back to your office?"

"Sure. I'm waiting on labs on Mrs. Miller, so I've got a minute."

Bill Thompson strode into the office chewing the last bite of a chocolate-covered donut and wiping the evidence off his fingers with a tissue. "Morning, Bro," he mumbled through chocolate goo. "I got your text. Are you done with our research project already?"

"More or less."

"Anything interesting?"

"Not really. I wish I could report something that would help your cause, but everything seems in order. I've made a huge worksheet on a long sheet of wrapping paper that I tacked to my office wall at the house. That way, I could visualize the entire picture. Why don't you come over tonight for dinner and we can go over it? I have a little research to finish up, but I'm pretty much done with it otherwise. Don't get your hopes up."

"OK. I'll be free any time after six."

"I'll let Nic know to set an extra plate. Say, six-thirty?"

"Perfect. See you then."

Bryce finished his clinic work and checked on his patients in the hospital, making it home just as Bill drove up to his house. They walked around to the back yard and admired the teeming gardens and were met on the deck by Nicole holding two glasses of chardonnay. "Cheers, gentlemen," she intoned as she handed them each a glass.

"None for you?" Bill asked, waiting for her to join them in a toast.

"No. Not tonight," she grinned and returned to the kitchen to finish preparing their meal.

Bryce led Bill to his office where he had reams of reports laid out on the desk as well as on a six-foot folding table that he had set up to lay out his research. Taped to the wall was an eight-foot piece of wrapping paper with heading names of the eight decedents, followed by notes under each heading specific to that case. "Here is the culmination of my two months of work, but I'm afraid it hasn't yielded many secrets. Anything that seemed out of the ordinary, even slightly, I noted on this worksheet in red, but I don't see any common denominators.

"Five of them died in the hospital, and one was briefly coded in the ER." He pointed to the far-left entry. "Number one died from hemorrhaging after surgery and number two from probable pneumonia and congestive heart failure and subsequent heart arrhythmia related to all the stress.

"Number three was an elderly guy with bone marrow failure. He stopped making white blood cells and died of severe weakness and overwhelming infection that he couldn't fight at the end. He barely made it to the hospital but didn't make it out of the ER."

Bryce moved a step to the right and pointed to the middle of the scroll. "Number four, here, died of shower emboli, multiple blood clots that float into the lungs, plugging them up and preventing blood flow and oxygenation.

"Number five was the interesting one. He died from tick paralysis, a rare disease that is only reported about once a year in North America. They get a tick embedded in a spot where it goes unnoticed, like the armpit or the groin or a fatty buttock fold. The tick feeds slowly, but while it feeds, it is continually releasing a toxin from its saliva that insidiously paralyzes the host muscles. If the tick is removed in time, the host can recover, but this one was missed deep in the groin up under the scrotum. The host died from paralysis of the respiratory muscles. Rare, but perfectly natural.

"Number six, the youngest of the group, was involved in a motorcycle accident and was pronounced dead at the scene. Positive blood alcohol, no full autopsy, signed out as obvious head and thoracic injuries.

"This one died from a heart attack and stroke after the stresses of surgery and an extremely low blood sugar. That's the Corsello case that we discussed a few weeks ago.

"And, of course, number eight was your last guy with the cocaine-induced heart arrhythmia. Here are my stacks of notes on each and the master scroll. I'll let you take them and drill down, see if you see something, but I've come up empty."

"Thanks, Bryce. I know how much time you spent on this, and I appreciate it more than you know."

"No problem. I just wish I had more to offer. Let's go eat before it gets cold."

7

ARRIVING AT THE HOSPITAL PARKING LOT AT DAWN TWO WEEKS later, Bryce recognized the slouching silhouette of his brother leaning against his car, the ever-present cup of coffee dangling in his huge hand. "Good morning, Detective Thompson. To what do I owe the pleasure of your company?"

"Couldn't sleep. I've been up nights reading over your reports. Or should I say trying to read your reports. Pretty heavy shit, half of which I don't understand."

"Sorry, I tried to put it in plain English."

"Oh! You did. It's just that there is so much science that I get lost. It reminded me of that time when you were in the fourth grade and figured out that the buoyancy of a body was positive when the lungs were full and negative when you exhaled. I remember watching you at the city pool, floating up, then sinking down, over and over, while you ran your experiments. I remember thinking at the time 'Who thinks about this shit?' but then I realized you always did, ever since you were old enough to talk.

"Anyway, the other night at your house, when you were summing up your findings, you used the word 'obvious' two or three times. Yet, there were no autopsies on two of those deaths, so the cause of death may seem obvious but is open to interpretation. Additionally, one of our decedents bled to death postoperatively, but your notes point out that there was only a limited autopsy performed. You put an asterisk by those notes in red ink. Why?"

Bryce gestured for Bill to walk with him as he tried to explain. "I'm not a pathologist, but it seemed like if hemorrhage was a suspected or even an obvious cause of death, a more extensive autopsy could have helped delineate underlying pathology further. If he died from post-op bleeding, was it the surgeon's fault due to sloppy technique? Or did the guy have an underlying clotting disorder that led to his demise? If there was a malpractice claim against the surgeon, that information could exonerate him. His pre-op labs were all OK, so he did not have any of the usual bleeding disorders. I checked with a pathologist friend at my alma mater at the University of Utah, and he said clotting studies postmortem are no good unless done STAT. Too much breakdown of proteins after death. But a more detailed autopsy would have shown what state the other organs were in. Was the bleeding only around the surgical anastomosis, or were multiple hemorrhages found? Were there multiple points of bleeding in multiple organs? We often give post-op patients a blood thinner called heparin to prevent clots. Did he get an accidental overdose?"

"Or an intentional overdose," Bill interjected.

"A trained forensics pathologist at the state medical examiner's lab might have done a heparin level, but it must be done right away, with fresh blood. We can't possibly know now."

"You also wrote 'Digoxin level?' on the seventy-two-year-old with heart failure, along with a big red question mark. Enlighten me."

"Well, this guy is older and has known heart failure, prior MI—sorry, prior heart attack—and was hospitalized for massive fluid retention. The nurses find him pulseless in the middle of the night, and CPR is unsuccessful. Open-and-shut case, right? However, I was looking at that one differently, thanks to you and your suspicious little mind. You're the one who told me he was married to his trophy wife thirty years his junior, and she stood to gain not only his millions in the bank but also his life insurance policy of six-point-five million. It got me thinking. What if she was giving him slow overdoses of digoxin in his food or drink? It's been reported before. There's actually a book about it. Slow accumulation causes slow degradation of certain bodily functions, and it could be written off to progressive aging and heart failure. Additionally, one of the side effects of digitalis toxicity is cardiac arrhythmia, erratic heartbeats that can mimic a heart attack. The heart stops moving blood efficiently and down they go. Not always fatal but often enough if they are frail to begin with."

"Wasn't that also one with a limited autopsy?"

"Yes. Autopsies are expensive, and unless there is reason to suspect foul play, they are often limited. No obvious trauma, no obvious needle marks, no surprises in the blood tests, bad heart, lungs full of fluid showing congestive heart failure. Open-and-shut."

"I'm still confused."

"It's open-and-shut if you see heart failure because you are looking for heart failure. We get blinders on when we have pre-conceived notions. We tend to see what we expect to see. Why look for a diagnosis when you already have a diagnosis? It's called anchoring.

"But one of the effects of digitalis toxicity is exacerbation of congestive heart failure and irregular heart rhythms. I'm guessing the pathologist didn't know he was on digitalis so didn't run the blood test. Dig wasn't on his computerized med list, but I talked to his pharmacist and found out that his attending physician called in a prescription for digoxin 0.25 milligrams daily. Phone prescriptions often don't make it into the electronic record, particularly if it happens after hours or on a weekend. And since it was not a legal case, no samples were saved in an evidence locker. It's probably nothing, but you asked me to mark anything that might be out of the ordinary. Digoxin is an old drug and not used much these days, so that was out of the ordinary. You got me to thinking, so I marked it."

"OK. But you've got me going down a pathway here that's keeping me awake at night. When a cop looks for patterns, he looks for motive and common denominators. There are two other common denominators. All the surgical deaths were post-op patients of Doctor Ray Littleton. But that only accounts for three cases, and what would any surgeon have to gain? Deaths on his service make him look incompetent. However, the pathologist on every single one of these cases was Doctor Antonio Malandra. And now your data implies that he's sloppy with his autopsies. Maybe he's not finding things because he's not looking for things?"

"Bill, you're barking up the wrong tree there. Ray is top drawer all the way. And Tony is smarter than almost anyone I know, and I know a lot of smart people. I've talked to him. He has a budget, like we all do. There's a shortage of pathologists, and the state medical examiner's office can't keep enough full-time pathologists on staff, not for what they pay, and we're lucky to have him. He's the only one of our pathologists who has the extra forensics training, so he subcontracts for the state instead of them having to transport all the bodies over to Missoula or Billings. But he can't do every test on every corpse every time. It would break the bank. He has protocols to follow. He has totally good reasons for the calls he has to make."

"You're probably right, but I wanted to share something else with you. While you were doing all this homework for me, I've been digging too. In my background checks on these decedents, all of them were having major problems in their married lives. There was either an affair going on, a separation, or rumors of impending divorce among their families and friends. Couple that with the fact that they were all heavily insured, and it makes a cop suspicious."

"I hear you, but a hunch and a proof are two different things."

"I know, but there's something else. Just how well do you know Doctor Malandra? Ever been to his house, gone flying with him, socialize with him?"

"Not really. As fellow pilots, we talk flying occasionally, but we don't socialize. Nic and I stay kind of to ourselves. Why?"

"The guy seems incredibly wealthy for his age. He has an elderly mother still living in upstate New York who he helps support, so I know he didn't inherit anything. Did you know he used to be married before he moved here?" He pulled a note card from his breast pocket. "Married a Jill Downing from Waterford, New York. A little town of 8,000 in upstate between Albany and Saratoga."

"You hear things. She died scuba diving, I guess."

"They were diving in South America when she disappeared. They never found the body, quit looking after several days, strong currents, coastal winds, assumed drowned and washed away. He collected over three million in life insurance."

"Doesn't that explain his financial status?"

"Only partially. He had to wait seven years to get his money since there was no body. I called over to Billings. Her parents fought him, accused him of abuse, said she had talked about not being happy, about leaving him. Then this timely diving accident. Makes you wonder. Also, he collects cars and flies an eight-passenger twin Piper worth around two million dollars. You fly your own plane. You scrimp and save to afford a used, four-passenger single-engine aircraft in a club with two other pilots. Explain that."

"Pathologists make a lot more than family docs, two or three times as much, maybe more, depending on how many hours they want to work, and Tony is a worker."

"He also has a home in the Bahamas and possibly a condo in Florida."

"You have been busy, haven't you?"

"Whatever. I'm going to question him about some of these autopsy things, but I won't tell him you've been helping me. I just wanted to give you a heads-up. I don't know if he knows we're related. I didn't want you to get blindsided."

"I appreciate that, Bill, but I still think you're barking up the wrong tree."

"I'm not the one barking. Your red pen led me down this path. You had it all laid out on that eight-foot spreadsheet. Tony Malandra is the only common link in all these cases. You're just too trusting. You think everyone is basically good. After doing this for twenty years, I think the human animal is basically flawed and will do about anything to get ahead, particularly if they think they won't get caught."

"I do think man is basically good. You've been a cop so long, you see the dirt on everything."

"I can prove you're wrong."

"How, pray tell?"

"If man was basically good, human behavior could follow ten simple rules, rules you could perhaps carve on two stone tablets. Instead, we have shelves of law books that fill a whole room and even they don't cover it all."

"Point made. But I'm still going to look at the positive side. Looking through your dark lens would drive a man to drink. As far as Tony Malandra is concerned, I don't know what you're thinking, but he is a born-again Christian, gives to charities, opposes abortion, and argues against the death penalty."

"Great. Then he won't mind talking to me. But there is one more coincidence that's bothering me. These high-insurance deaths started eight years ago. Doctor Malandra moved here from Billings ten years ago."

"As you said. Coincidence."

"Hey, I'll let you get to work. Sorry to take so much time. Thanks, again."

"No problem," Bryce said as he headed into the hospital. "Talk to you later."

That evening, as pink cirrus reflected a receding sun beyond the mountains, heralding warmer summer days to come, Bryce mowed the lawn and helped Nicole weed the flower beds, then headed in for a shower and a late dinner. "Bill came by this morning before rounds," he explained as he poured himself a glass of pinot grigio. "He has that insurance company investigation in his craw like a bulldog with a bone. I'm afraid he's getting tunnel vision. I mean, he wants so badly to find a crime, he might be forcing motives onto innocent occurrences. Today, he started talking about the surgeon and the pathologist as if they could be co-conspirators or something."

"Detectives think differently than normal people. We've known that for years. At least, I've known that since I met Bill."

Bryce extended an empty wine glass toward Nicole, eyebrows raised in that universal question mark.

"Not tonight, Hon." She shrugged and turned back toward the kitchen counter.

"Nothing new?" He asked hesitantly, afraid of jinxing their luck even though he didn't believe in jinxes, or luck.

"No news is good news. One day at a time is all I can hope for," she added as she plated their grilled trout and asparagus. "One day at a time."

"No spotting or cramping?" he asked as he walked up behind her and massaged her shoulders.

"Nothing at all. I feel great, Hon. Quit worrying. It'll happen. Sooner or later, it will happen."

"I love your positivity. I am the luckiest man in the world," he added as he hugged her and kissed the back of her neck. "Absolutely the luckiest."

8

SATURDAY DAWNED FULL AND BRIGHT. NICOLE'S PLOTS WERE bursting with growth, and her flower beds were more colorful than they could remember. They were trimming and weeding when Bill walked around the corner of the house, jaw clenched and lips pursed so tightly they paled. Bryce recognized the look.

"Hey. What's up?"

"Just a few questions," Bill said as Nicole continued on toward the back of the yard, affording them privacy.

"Shoot."

"How well do you know Doctor Malandra? I mean, is he a bit strange?"

"I guess I didn't think so. At least, no stranger than anyone who enjoys digging around in dead bodies and looking into a microscope all day. Why?"

"When I talked to him Tuesday, I lobbed softballs, loosening him up, developing a friendly rapport, and he was all "Yes, sir" and "No, sir" and helpful and pleasant. But when I went back on Thursday and started asking harder questions, the ones I really wanted to ask, he was acting all busy and preoccupied. Too busy to talk much. But that wasn't it. It was his body language. I'm sure he didn't expect a second visit. I caught him off guard. He wouldn't look me in the eye. And he seemed evasive when I started asking him about those missing autopsy findings, brushing them off like they were meaningless trivia. It wasn't what he said, it was how he said it."

"Maybe he was busy and irritated that you were bothering him again. Why did you go back on Thursday in the first place? Why didn't you do it all on Tuesday?"

"Technique."

"What?"

"It's my technique. Soften them up with easy stuff the first day. Get them to answer some simple, straightforward questions and establish some basic facts. Then see if they give different answers later. People who are telling the truth have no problem with that. But people who are being evasive can't keep all their lies straight. They start getting nervous. They hesitate. I don't know how to explain it, Bryce, but their body language usually tells me more than their words."

"Did he contradict himself?"

"Only once. On Tuesday, he said that the vitreous humor sample on the most recent death, that cocaine death, must have been lost. On Thursday, he said it wasn't taken because it wasn't needed. Cause of death was obvious. I know it doesn't sound like much, but it's there. It's an inconsistency, and I'm going to go to his place up in the hills today and talk with him again. It's one thing to talk to someone about business at their business, but going into their home territory can put them on the defensive. I want to see how he reacts."

"Anything specific?"

"Yes. That's why I wanted to talk to you first." Bill pulled a notebook from his jacket pocket. "In your report, the part about the patient who died of post-op hemorrhage, you circled 'PT and PTT Normal January 20th. Platelet Count Normal.' Then 'Routine Right Hemicolectomy January 21st.' Then 'Patient deceased January 23rd, cause of death Post-Op Hemorrhage.' Why was that marked in red?"

"You asked me to mark anything that didn't seem to fit. Those tests tell us that the patient had no bleeding tendencies, yet he had a belly full of blood two days later. Of course, it happens. We warn patients every time we take them to the OR that it's a possibility, even make them sign a form that they have been warned. The older they are, the higher the risk. But the guy wasn't that old, mid-sixties I think, and Ray Littleton is an excellent surgeon. Plus, the guy bled out so fast they didn't have time to take him back to the OR."

"Anything else?"

"No, but that's just the point. There was no mention of other organs being hemorrhagic. The belly was opened, and it was documented that it was full of blood and that the primary staple line had leaked, and the cause of death was obvious. But usually there is mention of the health of the other organs. They were only mentioned in passing as 'normal.'"

"OK. What does that mean in layman's terms?"

"I'm not positive. Maybe it's standard to do it this way in routine cases or limited autopsies, but in criminal cases, they dissect every organ and do toxicology and microscopic on everything."

"Routine," Bill interjected, "except the guy had a five-million-dollar life insurance policy payable to his wife. Routine, except the guy was screwing a twenty-something secretary down the hall."

"Ooooh!"

"Yeah. So, what was your point on this PT and PTT stuff?"

"Well, there were no blood-clotting studies on this guy immediately postmortem. Now, blood chemistry changes pretty quickly after death, and they would have to be done STAT, but it would have been interesting to see what they were. Like I told you a few weeks ago, a trained forensics specialist probably would have done a heparin level, but this was a limited autopsy. Remember, I said we usually thin people's blood slightly after major surgery or during prolonged bed rest to prevent clots in their legs or pelvis, clots that can break away and move to their heart or lungs. I just got to thinking that a nurse could have accidentally given too much blood thinner, which would cause the guy to bleed, but it wouldn't be discoverable in the chart audit because the nurse would have charted the dose they were supposed to give, not the dose they accidently gave."

"Interesting. How do we find out without asking Malandra himself?"

"I suppose you would have to exhume the body."

"Good luck with that one."

"What do you mean?"

"Bryce, every single one of these bodies was cremated. The evidence is gone. Up in smoke."

"Oh, shit."

"'Oh, shit' is right. Now do you see why I can't let this go? Any one case, any one thing here or there, would look coincidental, but putting pieces together over this time span, you begin to see the ten-thousand-piece puzzle start to have some form. I can't sleep at night mulling the permutations."

"Well, don't push yourself into an early heart attack."

"One more thing. I looked up Shower Emboli. You had that circled in red on that sixty-year-old. Multiple blood clots showering the lungs, plugging them, cutting off blood flow through the lungs. You marked 'Source?' with a big red question mark behind it. I want to ask him about that, but I want to be sure I have this straight. What source?"

"Shower emboli have to come from somewhere. There was no mention of 'venous thrombosis' anywhere else. Venous thrombosis means blood clots, usually starting in the large veins of the legs or pelvis. These can break off and float into the lungs. I just thought it could have been an oversight, but that isn't like Tony Malandra. So, I got to thinking, what if the guy had been given the wrong type of blood, an incompatible blood match? It happens, and it's often fatal, and the hospital pays up. But if no one knows about it, there is no query. No lawsuit. Just another post-op death due to blood clots, which are more common than people know."

"That's what I thought," Bill said. "I just wanted to make sure I was reading that right. Suppose he is given a pint of blood, not by

48

accident, but on purpose, and it's old, partially-clotted blood pushed into his IV line by someone who stands to make a couple of million dollars if the guy conveniently dies? The wife pulled in a neat four mil on that one. Would they have been able to trace a wrong blood type?"

"He was only given one pint. Nurses are required to have a second nurse sign a form that the blood was double-checked and was the right type. Everything checked out."

"I know. But suppose he was given a second pint? Suppose someone slipped into his room in the middle of the night and gave him the wrong blood on purpose. Someone who could have slipped into another patient's room and given an overdose of insulin a couple of years ago? Someone who could then cover his own tracks by doing a sloppy autopsy? Someone who is far too rich for his age? Someone who has flown to Switzerland twice in the last eight years? Someone whose name keeps coming up on every single case?"

"Good lord. No wonder you can't sleep at night. Twenty years of chasing bad guys has you thinking strange thoughts."

"You cannot imagine."

"So, what's next?"

"I need another favor. I need you to think like a cop this weekend, Bryce. I need you to quit trying to defend the medical community and go through these cases again and, with your medical knowledge, assume there's been a crime. See what scenario fits if there is someone who knows medicine and is up to no good. Don't think like Bryce Thompson. Think like Bill Thompson. Think that every sleazeball out there is trying to get rich quick. Think how you would have done it and how you would have covered your tracks. See what you can come up with from your medical perspective. Be diabolical."

"OK, but I'm afraid maybe you want that new job so badly you're bending facts to fit the scenario in your head. I worry that you are preoccupied with this to the point where you might be seeing a crook behind every tree."

"Bryce, there is a crook behind every tree," he said as he started off. "There's something not right here, and this pathologist is the one common link. You're the one who pointed that out. I need to talk to him one more time, see if there are any more inconsistencies. With all the bodies cremated, he's my last link. I'm heading out to his place, and I'm going to push him. I'm going to make him sweat and see if he contradicts himself again. No matter how smart they are, they can't make up enough lies to cover all the lies they've already laid out. There's a hundred ways to catch a crook, Bryce, and if they're a genius, they might think of ninety-nine of them. Wish me luck."

"Okay, but be careful. I'll go through each case this weekend and get, what did you say, diabolical. I'll make notes and get them to you Monday. And don't tell him you're my brother."

"Of course. Thanks, man. Again."

Bill disappeared around the corner of the house as Nicole came back to Bryce's side. He was looking vacantly toward the mountains, thinking about what had just gone down. Sensing the wheels turning in his head, Nicole gently laid her head against his arm. "Relax, Hon. Try not to work today. You've been working too hard. You don't have to work all the time."

"I know. Later. As soon as this is behind us. I promise. Later, we'll have more time. Then we can relax and enjoy life."

By Sunday evening, Bryce had gone over all the medical records again. It wasn't that difficult since he had been living with them in his head for weeks. But this time, he tried to do what Bill said. He tried to be diabolical and imagine he was trying to harm someone with his medical knowledge in a way that would not be traceable. He gave Bill a call late Sunday evening.

Bill answered on the first ring. "Hey, Bro. What's up?"

"I went over the cases again like you said. I put myself in the shoes of a crook who knows medicine. I hate to admit it, but you were right. Most of those cases could be rigged.

"There are a lot of drugs that cause agranulocytosis, extremely low white blood cell counts that set you up for infection. If that elderly guy with bone marrow failure was being given one of those drugs, it would look like a typical elderly disease process. Squirting a syringe full of heparin into an IV line could make a post-op patient bleed out. Pushing a syringe full of old, incompatible blood into an IV line could cause shower emboli. Cocaine injected into a drunk or drugged guy who was passed out could easily finish him off. Injecting an overdose of insulin would definitely drop someone's blood sugar to near zero, causing a stroke or heart attack."

"I knew it. There's something not right about this Malandra. When I went up to his place on Saturday, he acted weird. Then he tried to confuse me by using nothing but polysyllabic medical terms that he thought would lead me off the scent. It was bizarre, his monologue. Maybe that's how pathologists talk to pathologists, but it was eerie the way he tried to obfuscate. What about the other two?"

"A motorcycle accident is a motorcycle accident, unless his bike was tampered with. But the last one, the tick paralysis, that's just too rare to be a set up. I don't see how that would be possible, but the others are open for discussion. I've made notes, and I'll send them over with Nicole in the morning. You'll be at home?"

"Yes. I'll wait for her. Thanks, Bryce. I'll take you both out to dinner next weekend as a small payback for all you've done."

9

MONDAY MORNING STARTED OFF LIKE ANY MONDAY MORNING. Too little sleep. Too much work. Too much worry. Bill's instructions had haunted Bryce all weekend, and what little sleep he did get was fretful. Bryce had made pages of notes, but their context was so foreign. Thinking like a criminal and realizing how much damage one could do with intentional misuse of physiology and pharmacology disturbed him. He showered quickly and grabbed a cup of coffee to drink on the way to the hospital.

"Nic, I need a favor. I've got a full schedule today, and I promised to get these notes to Bill. Can you drop them off at his house? He said he would wait at the house for you."

"Sure. I have to go downtown anyway."

"Thanks. Love you," he said as he kissed her goodbye.

"Always," she added as she returned the kiss, a habit never broken.

Hospital rounds were quick, with only two in-patients, and Bryce was busy at the clinic mid-morning when his secretary came back to his office, a worried look on her face. "Doctor, there are two policemen here to see you. They said they work with your brother. Can I bring them back?"

"Of course."

The two plainclothes officers came down the hallway, not a smile to be seen. Entering the office and closing the door behind them, the taller of the two spoke. "Doctor Thompson, I am Detective Willett, and this is my assistant, Detective Shopp. Doctor, please have a seat."

"Why? What's happened?" But he really didn't have to ask. He knew from their demeanor it was bad news before the words were uttered. He sank into the chair and clutched the armrests, his mind tumbling over the range of possibilities like an empty boat tumbling through white water.

"Bill did not report in today, and he wasn't answering his phone, so I sent a squad car over for a routine wellness check. They found him lying inside the entryway to his front door. He had been dead for over an hour."

Stunned, Bryce slumped back into his chair as his whole body sagged under the weight of the news. He tried to talk but his voice failed him, his mouth so dry he could not get his tongue to work. He took a sip of water. "I knew he was working too hard and not sleeping well. But I never dreamed this. Heart attack, I assume? No sign of foul play?"

"Doctor, it would look like a routine heart attack under ordinary circumstances, and I have no doubt that was what it was intended to look like. But these are not ordinary circumstances. I don't know how to tell you this," he said as he dabbed his eye, "but your wife was there." He paused and cleared his throat. "She is deceased as well. Both were found lying in the hallway inside the front door. No signs of trauma. No weapons. No violence. No forced entry."

"No! Oh ... God ... I asked her to ..." Bryce choked on the words as the tears rolled down his cheeks. He tried again. Choked again. Took another sip of water. "I ... I asked her to drop some papers off for Bill this morning," Bryce said, his voice a hollow monotone. "I sent her there."

"Yes. There were medical papers scattered about in the entryway."

"I sent her there. I sent her to her death." Color deserted Bryce's face as he swooned, head spinning.

Detective Willett took a quick step toward Bryce and put a hand on his shoulder to steady him. He gave him a minute, then added. "I don't need to tell you that two people don't drop dead of a heart attack in the same room at the same instant by chance. We are running chemical analysis on everything in that hallway. We instituted HAZMAT protocols immediately. Once the area is cleared for toxins, we will need you to come downtown and make final identification of the bodies for the death certificates."

"No! I can't. I won't."

"But, Doctor, you are their only living relative. At least you are Bill's only living relative. It's legal protocol."

"No. You know Bill as well as anyone. You can do it. I will not have that be my last picture of them. I won't."

"But …"

"I will not do it. When I was thirteen, a drunk driver killed my parents. To this day, I cannot get a mental picture of them alive and happy and smiling. The only image that comes into my mind's eye is of them lying cold and pale and swollen in those caskets. That will not be the last image I have of my only family. I will not do it."

"I see. We'll work something out. You do understand we will need to order autopsies?"

Bryce jerked upright. "They must be done in Missoula, not here. I want them done by the state's chief medical examiner."

Willett glanced at Detective Shopp, shrugged slightly, then turned back to Bryce. "Of course. Whatever you say."

Bryce tried to say something, but he couldn't seem to hear his own voice. He felt like he was in a deep, dark cellar and the door was closing.

"Doctor. There is one more thing you will need to know."

"What else can there possibly be?"

"Your wife was pregnant. She aborted as she died. I am going to investigate this as a triple homicide."

That was when the door slammed shut on Bryce Thompson's life.

10

THERE IS THAT TWILIGHT PERIOD EVERY PERSON EXPERIENCES in the seconds or minutes just before sleep extinguishes thought, seconds where reality and dream float together as a oneness, neither dream nor real. Bryce Thompson floated in that twilight realm for the next three days as he tried to talk with the funeral home people, make plans for services with Nicole's parents, compose obituaries, arrange seating, arrange flowers, arrange things that didn't matter to anyone beyond the funeral directors in their attempts to make the unmanageable manageable. They started to lead him into the casket room, and he stopped abruptly at the doorway.

"No! No caskets. They both wanted cremation. Once the bodies have been released by the ME, they will be cremated. No lying underground for a thousand years as food for worms. If we are but dust to dust, then let it be done. I will spread their ashes in a field of wildflowers where their atoms can go back into the cycle of life."

He turned away from the door to the casket room as the assistant funeral director said, "We have some beautiful urns you can choose from."

"It doesn't matter. I just told you; a wildflower field will be their resting place." He walked away as the soft-spoken gentleman tried to explain, finally giving up when Bryce walked out of the building and headed for home.

The summer sun was settling over Nicole's gardens as Bryce walked into the house, dreading the silence, dreading the horrible loneliness he knew awaited him. He opened the Wine Captain and retrieved the expensive bottle of pinot grigio that Nicole had bought him for Father's Day, making love to him and saying, "Here's hoping!" Was that the night she conceived? He would never know.

He popped the cork, took out an oversized wine glass, filled it to the brim, and walked out into the back yard, bottle in hand. The evening was perfect. Perfect temperature. Perfect breeze. Perfect view. Perfect sunset. Perfectly hollow. Bryce drained the glass and refilled it. He plucked several Roma tomatoes—tomatoes that had so carefully been tended by the gentlest hands in the world. He sat in the deck chair, ate the fruit, and then drained the second glass. He could feel the buzz coming on as he poured a third. He polished off the bottle in less than thirty minutes, then retrieved a bottle of sauvignon blanc and did it equal justice. Opening his third bottle, he started to cry again as he sunk into the abyss, the seemingly endless Hades his life had become, his entire body engulfed by the waves of emotion that crashed over him as he sobbed himself into total exhaustion.

His throbbing headache was the first thing Bryce noticed as it awakened him from his slumber in the deck chair at first light. His neck was stiff and his back sore from the awkward slump he was in when he had finally slipped into unconsciousness. He went inside, took four ibuprofen tablets, and stepped into the shower. Dressing quickly, he went back to the funeral home and, with Nicole's parents' help, made final arrangements. He muddled through the day and the prayer services that evening, and, unable to think of food, excused himself early from a dinner with Nicole's family and friends at the hotel restaurant. Bryce returned to his house and repeated the previous evening's ritual, knowing not what else to do, knowing not how to go on.

A triple funeral service was held the following day. The church overflowed. The entire police force and medical community, along with Nicole's family and countless friends, filled the pews. There was no one who met Nicole who didn't adore her. The luncheon afterward was filled with handshakes and hugs and thousands of kind words, but Bryce could not have told anyone whom he had seen or talked with, still floating in his twilight of grief and disbelief.

When the last guests were gone, he took the three mahogany urns and drove into the mountains to a national forest area that he knew would never be developed. He opened his backpack and placed each urn inside, reading the names slowly out loud. "Bill." "Nicole." He picked up the tiny, palm-sized urn. "George William." He read the name she had picked over a year ago to honor both Nicole's father and Bryce's surrogate father should their first-born be a boy. He donned the pack, grabbed a small shovel, and hiked to the top of the meadow that burst into color each spring. It was a gently sloping vale where he and Nicole often came to hike or picnic and escape the heat, a place he could drive to easily in the future when he wanted to visit their final resting place. He made his way slowly upslope as he sprinkled Bill's ashes along the west side, then whispered his final goodbyes, each with another tear as he gently sprinkled Nicole's ashes intermixed with baby George's ashes down the east side. Lastly, he took the shovel and buried the urns near the trailhead, their funeral complete. Bryce stood and looked out over the meadow one last time. He said goodbye, promising them he would visit every spring when they bloomed into wildflowers, then headed back to town.

Bryce knew he needed sleep, but he did not need a third hangover. After dinner with Nicole's family and them saying their goodbyes, he readied himself for bed, then took a double dose of some leftover Ambien that they had used to combat jet lag on their trip to France. He crawled into Nicole's side of the bed and buried his head into the residual scent of her perfume as he cried himself to sleep.

11

THE GRAY HAZE OF DAWN HAD GIVEN WAY TO BRIGHT SUN AS Bryce made his way to the hospital the next morning. Wrinkled and unshaven, he strode into the pathology department.

"Where's Malandra? I need to talk to him."

"He's not here, Doctor Thompson," the secretary replied. "He had to fly out to New York on short notice. His mother is ill. We aren't sure when he'll be back."

"Not here? When did he leave?"

"Last Saturday or Sunday, I think. He left a note for the week-end crew and flew out in his plane."

Bryce left the department and walked to his clinic. He instructed the staff to cancel patients until further notice. After dropping Nicole's parents at the airport and seeing them off, he headed for the police station and sought out Detective Willett.

"Good morning, Doctor Thompson. I am so sorry for your loss. I can't imagine what you are going through. I hope you know how much everyone, and I do mean everyone, in the force admired and respected Bill. He was one of the smartest cops we've ever had. I'm sure you have a thousand questions. What can I help you with?"

"Any information from your HAZMAT team? Any poisons, toxins, any source, anything at all?"

"I'm sorry, but it's much too soon. Chemical analysis will take days to weeks, as I'm sure you know. But, no, we have no clue as to the source. Carbon monoxide has been ruled out, but you probably guessed that. Carbon monoxide usually gets sleepers, not two people who are up on their feet and active."

"Can I go to the scene? See if I can help find any clues?"

"I'm sorry, Doctor. That would break protocol. I know you need answers, but you are not trained in the field of investigation, and although you mean well, you could contaminate evidence. Additionally, you are technically a person of interest even though we have corroborated your whereabouts on Monday. You were at the hospital by 6:30 a.m. and at your clinic immediately after that until we came to talk to you. Time of death has been established as approximately 9 a.m., which fits with what you told us about your wife's plans for the day."

"I'm a person of interest?" The air left his lungs in a decrescendo sigh. "Of course, I am. Most women are killed by their husbands or boyfriends, aren't they?"

"Ninety-three percent to be exact."

"Is there anything, anything at all, I can help with?"

"Actually, there is. I have a file packed with pictures from the scene. You could look them over and see if you see anything out of the norm. I can set up a sub-file with no pictures of the deceased in them. It will take a few minutes to move the files. Go back there," he said, pointing to the back corner of the offices. "Grab some coffee and a breakfast bar while I do this. You look like you could use a cup about now."

"Sounds good, Detective. Thanks."

Minutes later, Bryce was at Willett's desk clicking through pictures of Bill's house and entryway. Within two minutes, he signaled to Willett.

"What is it, Doc?"

"This briefcase lying in the entryway. It shouldn't be there."

"How can you be sure?"

"I sent my notes over with Nicole in a large manila envelope. Besides, we don't have one like that, and Bill didn't own a hard briefcase. He carried a large, soft, calfskin satchel that I gave him for his birthday several years ago. He used the shoulder strap. He hated briefcases. He said a cop should always have both hands free in case of trouble. Check that thing out." He went through the files a second time, but that was the only thing he saw out of the ordinary. They compared notes for several minutes, then Bryce left for home. He couldn't wait for the police. It was time to start his own investigation.

12

RYCE HAD NEVER BEEN TO TONY MALANDRA'S HOME IN THE mountains. Malandra wasn't the type to invite people out for a staff social or Christmas party. He kept to himself and traveled extensively. Bryce knew the general area where Malandra lived, but this was the last place Bill said he was going to that fateful Saturday to question Malandra. Bill had mentioned the road he had to take to get to the dead-end lane that led into Malandra's property. Once he found the road on his GPS, it was a quick drive up the winding, gravel road to the multilevel, brick and glass home hidden high in the forest. Bryce rang the doorbell several times and knocked on every door, but there was no response, only the deathly quiet of the place belying any presence of life. He tried each door, but they were all locked. He tried to open any windows he could reach, but they were likewise secure. Through the windows, he could see over a dozen trophy mounts from North America, Russia, New Zealand, and Africa. He knew that big-game hunting was one of the reasons Malandra had moved to Montana. He thought of breaking a window but decided that he was not going to start the day with breaking and entering.

The three-stall attached garage looked like any other garage, save for its contents. Looking through a small window, he could see a brand-new Porsche 718 Boxster and what looked like a Lamborghini Spyder parked inside. Tool benches with tools neatly arranged against the back wall rounded out the picture. The two-stall detached garage was locked, as it should be with an immaculately restored 1944 Packard and an equally pristine 1927 Ford Model T seen through the tiny windows in the overhead doors. He walked around the property and checked out the fifteen-by-thirty garden shed. It was locked as well, and through the windows all he could see were a riding mower and a beat-up pickup full of firewood, various pieces of lawn equipment, tools, scrap lumber, and odd miscellany. The rest of the property seemed devoid of structure or other interest but was well cared for and neat with at least eight cords of firewood perfectly stacked near the back of the house for easy retrieval in the winter months.

Dejected and empty-handed, Bryce started for his truck when he glanced up the mountainside and caught a glint of sunlight reflecting off a shiny metallic object, the rays just peeking through the heavy growth of timber. *Probably nothing, but I came all this way. Might as well check it out.*

It was a steep climb, but the rocky soil was well-packed, and the path had little growth on it. It was used frequently enough. He followed the trail as it twisted between the trees, and there he saw the top of an old, weathered shed hidden behind an outcropping of rock that sheltered the depression the shed was built into. The only sign of its existence from below was the metal chimney that had glinted in the sunlight, betraying its seclusion.

Bryce circled the shed, but there were no windows to lend insight into the shed's contents. As he rounded the back, he passed downwind and caught a stench that made him involuntarily hold his breath and exhale to avoid further insult to his olfactory nerves. The smell of rotting animal flesh was unmistakable to any outdoorsman. He decided it was time for breaking and entering after all.

The door had a rickety fifty-year-old handle, but a newer hasp and padlock were installed above it. Bryce trotted down the trail to his pickup and retrieved his Leatherman multi-tool and made his way back to the shed. The wood was old, weathered, and porous, and it didn't take long to pry the edge of the hasp up and progressively loosen its four screws. Within a few minutes, he had the screws pried out. He opened the door, but the stench stopped him momentarily. It did more than attack his nose. It stuck to his skin and tried to insinuate itself into his pores. He wafted the door back and forth, forcing clean air to mix with the dead. After a minute, he took a deep breath and entered the shed.

In the back of the shed was a huge, glass-enclosed terrarium, and inside he could see the skull of a large black bear amid at least a thousand dermestid beetles. The skull was nearly devoid of flesh, the clean white bone shining in the dark interior. The beetles were doing what came naturally, eating anything that was edible, which to a dermestid beetle is everything except bone. Muscle, tendon, ligament and sinew—it was all food for these hungry critters, and taxidermists had known this for decades. The taxidermy fraternity had used this knowledge to popularize the European mount, or skull mount, rather than the traditional fur mount, which collected insects and dust and eventually fell apart. In a corner of the terrarium sat a quart bottle with a dozen tiny holes drilled in the lid to allow airflow for a score of ticks getting their blood meal from a slab of meat.

In the near corner of the shed stood an old wood stove, and on a shelf in the back, he noticed a trophy deer skull next to a huge caribou skull. Everyone knew Malandra was an avid hunter, but he had never mentioned taxidermy being a hobby. Seeing nothing else of interest, Bryce exited the shed, pounded the hasp screws back into place, and left for town.

13

THE NEXT SEVERAL DAYS DRAGGED ON LIKE A SLOW-MOTION dream. Bryce could not concentrate on anything productive, his thoughts constantly circling back to what could kill his wife and brother, two perfectly healthy people, in a matter of seconds. The preliminary autopsy findings were inconclusive but were consistent with respiratory arrest, a sudden cessation of breathing followed by cardiac standstill. Had Bill been alone, it would easily have passed as a middle-aged, over-worked, over-stressed detective dying of a heart attack. But the presence of a younger female in perfect health put the lie to that scenario. Only some type of rapidly acting toxin could do that. They didn't even have time to move from the hall inside the doorway or make a call.

Bryce had tried to call Malandra's cell phone over a dozen times without luck. Granted, Bill had sent many a lowlife to prison and had plenty of enemies, but Malandra was probably the last person to have seen Bill alive. Now he had magically disappeared. Bryce needed to talk to him, and preferably in person, remembering what Bill had said about his body language. No one in the pathology department had a clue where in New York his mother lived. Malandra was too closemouthed for that. So, frustrating as it was, all Bryce could do was wait until he returned to Montana.

The following Tuesday, he received a text from Detective Willett and drove down to the police station. "Good morning, Detective. You said you had some news? Cause of death? Toxicology?"

"Nothing definite yet, but you told me to check out that briefcase, and you were right. It had no fingerprints on it except Bill's and Nicole's. Inside were some old newspapers. No prints on those either. So, I am thinking that it was left for Bill to find, only Nicole picked it up and brought it inside when she delivered your package, which would explain her prints on the handle."

"Go on."

"The key to this puzzle was in the briefcase, not in its contents. You see, the inside front wall had been modified, and inside the hasp on the right-hand side was a tiny CO_2 cartridge. It was superglued inside the lock compartment up against the spring-arm of the lock. The CO_2 had been expelled and replaced with a toxin, then re-pressurized and sealed with superglue. When the button was pushed, a tiny pin punctured the seal and released the gas. What little residue was detected has led the chemists to believe it was a form of sarin, a highly lethal poison that is easily aerosolized. Or it could be a form of VX, which is ten times more potent than sarin. It was used in the Japanese subway massacre by the doomsday cult Aum Shinrikyo and implicated in the killing of Kim Jong Un at Kuala Lumpur Airport."

There it was. The gut-wrenching truth of what killed his family. The chill ran down his entire body, the hair on his arms erect. Bryce couldn't respond at first. After a few deep breaths, he was able to reply. "We studied that in organophosphate toxicology. I believe it was developed as a pesticide in the fifties but turned out that it was too deadly to use around humans or livestock."

"Yes. That's exactly why it was banned by the international weapons convention of 1997. But apparently it isn't that hard to brew up if you know your chemistry and have the lab equipment and know-how. Most bad guys who have tried to brew it up in their kitchen labs have wound up killing themselves."

The answer to the *what* now began to solidify Bryce's suspicion of the *who* in this twisted equation. "That is precisely the point, Detective. A typical bad guy in a kitchen lab is one thing, but how about a very smart bad guy with a huge lab at his disposal? How about a very brilliant bad guy with all the resources and all the medical knowledge needed to not only do it but also to make it look like a natural death?"

"Okay. What are you getting at?"

"Doctor Malandra was the last person Bill was going to see that weekend. He had been questioning him about some autopsy findings that seemed out of the norm, and he was suspicious something was up."

"Seriously? Malandra does a lot of our forensic work. He's the best there is. People from at least a five-state area request his opinion on tough cases. He's like Mr. Law and Order to us."

"I know that. I actually told Bill the very same thing that weekend. But look at the facts. Bill questions Malandra three times that week, 'pushes him' was how he put it, then ends up dead the following Monday. Malandra conveniently leaves town, supposedly the day before, to cover his alibi. Figure those odds. Additionally, he has the whole hospital lab at his disposal. Bottom line, we need to get into the hospital's pathology lab and search for more clues."

"I need probable cause. I have no grounds for a search warrant."

"I just outlined a probable cause for you. Why did he so conveniently disappear?"

"You told me yourself that he has a sick mother in New York. Wouldn't you go if your mother was sick?"

"Of course, I would. If only I had a mother. But the constellation of events is too far beyond the pale to simply ignore. My family has been murdered, and Tony Malandra is our only link. You said you were going to investigate it like a triple homicide. Those were the words you used. So, let's investigate."

"I'm sorry, Doc, it's not that simple. Besides, Doctor Malandra is a friend to this department. You're asking too much. Let's wait for him to come back to town, then I'll sit down and talk with him, and you'll see that there is a perfectly logical explanation for everything."

"Of course, there will be a logical explanation. Smart people plan ahead."

"You are hurting and want answers. I know that, but we can't let emotion set the course of an investigation. We'll settle this when he's back in town."

"And if I file a formal complaint against him?"

"You could do that. Then the chief and the county attorney would have to make the call. But, just to warn you, it might not get past the chief's desk, let alone the county attorney's. That's just how the system works."

"Or doesn't work," Bryce quipped as he turned to go. "Thanks for your time, Detective."

"Put yourself in my shoes. What if he was saying these same things about you? What if he said you killed your wife for the insurance money? I wouldn't arrest you just on someone's insinuation. I would have to investigate. Evaluate. Corroborate."

"I'm not asking you to arrest him. I'm just asking you to get a warrant and look around his place. If everything is copacetic, then fine. But at least you'll know you tried."

"I'll think about it. But no promises."

"I guess that's all I can ask. Thanks, Detective." With that, Bryce left headquarters and headed home. He changed clothes and collected a few articles he thought might come in handy, then he called Jerry's Lock and Key.

"Jerry's," a sweet voice answered on the second ring. "How may we help you?"

"Hello. This is Doctor Tony Malandra, and I have lost my house keys and am in a terrible bind. I need to gather up some things and be back at the hospital somewhat urgently. Can I have you meet me at my property and get me into the house?"

"Sure, doctor. I can have a man on the road in minutes."

Bryce gave her the address and headed for the hospital.

14

BRYCE WALKED QUICKLY TO THE PATHOLOGY DEPARTMENT AND went directly to Malandra's office. As the secretary was explaining that Doctor Malandra had still not returned, Bryce was palming a few of Malandra's business cards. Thanking her for her trouble, he exited the building and headed for the house on the mountainside.

He drove as fast as he dared, needing to beat the locksmith there to avoid suspicion. He parked in front of the empty stall he had identified in his earlier scouting trip, hoping to make it look like his vehicle was supposed to be there. He had barely exited his pickup when a minivan pulled up, brightly adorned with Jerry's Lock & Key logos.

"Thank you for coming so quickly," he said as he shook hands with the young man. "Are you Jerry?"

"Yes, doctor. Owner and sole employee. That was my wife who answered the phone. We're trying to make a go of it so she can quit her other job and work with me full time, maybe get a retail outlet in a good location to get into some sales. It's not as easy to start your own business as some trade school teachers make it sound."

Bryce reached into his hip pocket and retrieved his wallet. "Here's my card," he said as he handed him Malandra's business card. "And I hope this will cover your expenses," he added as he handed him three crisp one-hundred-dollar bills.

"Oh, that's too much," Jerry blushed as he looked at more money than he made in many slow weeks.

"Believe me, you are saving my butt. It's a long drive up here, and it will be worth it if I can get my stuff and get back to the hospital in short order. It's worth every penny for your promptness and your trouble."

The bonus payment made the impressionable young locksmith forget about any secondary proof of identity. He pocketed the money and grabbed his tool bag as he walked to the front door. "So, your garage door opener failed, huh?"

Bryce was caught off guard with that remark. Recovering quickly, he stammered, "Yeah. The perfect storm. Forget your keys and forget to replace the damn battery. I knew it was getting weak because yesterday I had to pull right up to the door before it would open, but today it had nothing."

"I know. Those little button batteries seem to go all at once," Jerry said as he toyed with the dead bolt. "They don't have the reserve of those older, heavier, nine-volt models," he added as they heard a firm click, and the door swung open. "There you go."

"Wow! You definitely are a pro. Thanks again," Bryce said, stepping inside like he owned the place. He watched until the minivan pulled away, then pulled two vinyl gloves from his pocket and donned them before he closed the door. No prints, he reminded himself.

He made quick work of the main-floor search, opening doors and drawers but not disrupting anything inside. He found nothing of interest and walked up the massive, curved stairway to the second floor. There was nothing particularly interesting in any of the bedrooms, and the office was neat but revealed little. He was careful not to leave any sign of his presence, but a cautious look through the contents of the drawers did not relinquish any clues to a secret pastime. He found no address book, which could give away the mother's address in New York, assuming Malandra even had a mother in New York. The large, locked, center desk drawer probably held anything that was of value. He couldn't pry that open without leaving marks, so he turned off the lights and went to the basement.

The basement was like any other basement, cool, damp, and uninteresting, although it seemed small for such a huge house. Woodworking tools and painting supplies, along with multiple cans of paint, lacquer, and varnish, graced one wall while a washer and drier graced another. Storage rooms held little other than a few pieces of old furniture and dusty animal mounts. With nothing out of the ordinary, Bryce sensed defeat. He was about to head back upstairs when he noticed marks on the concrete floor. Scratch marks on cement are common, but they are usually linear. These were curved and seemed out of place as they swerved across the back of the basement floor in a perfect arc in front of a wall of shelves. Books, tools, and miscellaneous odds and ends lined the shelves.

Bryce didn't really think about it. His sixth sense told him something didn't fit. Crouching low, he could see the wheels that were scribing the marks on the floor. As he examined the bookcase, it only took a few seconds to notice that the dust was worn off the right end of the middle shelf, while the other shelves had a uniform patina of dust. He felt around under that shelf and detected a metallic latch. Pulling up on the latch, he heard a click and felt the wall jog. Pulling on the shelf, the entire wall unit swung away on hidden wheels, revealing a small laboratory with dozens of beakers, pipettes, graduated cylinders and partially filled chemical bottles. In the middle of the workbench was a glass-enclosed chemistry fume hood with an industrial-grade exhaust fan.

"Son of a bitch! He could concoct some bad shit here." Talking out loud to himself, Bryce was dumfounded at his discovery. "And I was implying to Willett that he had the resources of the hospital lab at his disposal, but it is staffed around the clock. He's too smart for that." He checked all around without touching anything, knowing how deadly the poison from the briefcase had been. He quickly snapped a dozen pictures and hoped they would not incriminate him for his illegal entry. Seeing a powdery residue on a portion of the workbench, he scraped some into a spare vinyl glove and tied it tightly, then headed for the city.

15

THE FOLLOWING MORNING, BRYCE DROVE DOWN TO HEADQUARTERS and sought out Detective Willett. "I know who killed my family." He took out a thumb drive and handed it to Willett. "Pull up those pictures."

Willett did as directed. "Okay, what am I looking at?"

"Tony Malandra has a secret chemistry lab in his basement and can concoct the sort of nerve agent that could kill two people instantly where they stood." He pulled a plastic bag containing the glove and powder out of his pocket and handed it to Willett. "I found this chemical in his lab. Can you have it analyzed and see if anything comes up that would connect it to my family's murder? And now can we get a search warrant for his house and property?"

"Wow!" Willett looked at Bryce, eyes searching. "But how did you get in?"

"I went up to talk to Malandra. He wasn't there, but there was an unlocked door, so I went in to take a peek. No broken windows. No forced entry. You have my word on that."

"I'll see what the lab comes up with, then we'll talk."

Early the next morning, Bryce received a call from Detective Willett. "The lab says that the residue in that container is not conclusive but could possibly be a forerunner to a stronger organophosphate chemical. You may have something here after all, Doctor Thompson."

"I know I have. People don't have chemical labs with sealed fume hoods and exhaust fans in their basements to make salsa. Let's get a search warrant and see what else we can come up with."

"I'll see what I can do. Come down to headquarters around three this afternoon, and we'll talk."

Bryce walked into headquarters at 2:55 p.m. and made his way to Willett's desk. "Any luck?"

"I'm afraid not, Doc. The chief would like to talk with you." Willett led Bryce into Chief Murphy's office.

"Good afternoon, Doctor Thompson. Have a seat. Coffee?"

"No, thanks."

"Willett has filled me in on your little investigation, but I'm afraid we can't act on it."

"Why is that? That chemical residue is at least consistent with organophosphate synthesis. And the pictures show that he could be making it right in his basement. Who has a fume hood in their home?"

"Well, for starters, you have no corroborating witnesses. Those pictures could have been taken anywhere. How do I know they weren't taken in your basement? Additionally, he was out of town when Bill died. It's your word against his. Furthermore, how did you get the alleged evidence?"

"Malandra was the last person my brother talked to before he was poisoned. He had been investigating his activities related to some other deaths. I went up to Malandra's place in the mountains to talk to him. A door was unlocked, so I went in thinking I would find him. That's when I came across a laboratory setup in his basement, a lab that would allow him to concoct the type of poison needed to kill my family so efficiently. I know it was him. Just get a search warrant, and I'll prove it to you."

"I'm sorry, but we can't take this to a judge without some sort of corroborating evidence. What else do you have?"

"Isn't the chemical enough?"

"It's unlikely it would be admissible in court. It could have come from anywhere. There is another problem, though. It is known in legal circles as the fruits of a poisonous tree. Technically, you were trespassing. If the original entry was illegal, any evidence downstream of the illegal activity is inadmissible. Do you have anything else? Any witnesses?"

Caught off guard, Bryce didn't know what to say without incriminating himself or the locksmith. "No, I have no witnesses. Just my own observations."

Chief Murphy stared at Bryce for a long moment. "Essentially, you were trespassing on private property, made illegal entry without permission, which amounts to invasion of privacy, and you want me to go to a judge to get a search warrant based on potentially illegal activity? Doctor, we have laws to protect people's rights for a reason. How would you like it if someone just waltzed into your house, planted, say, a child porn video on your computer or a kilo of cocaine under your headboard, then called the police demanding a search warrant? If we only obey the laws that are convenient, then there is no law."

"I'll grant you that. So, how do I make a citizen's arrest? I heard from one of my nurses that he's back in town as of last night. I'm going to nail this bastard."

"You'll need a lot more evidence, and better evidence, than you have now. Look! You are distraught and emotional over your loss. I understand that. But I'm afraid that emotion is clouding your logic. You're cutting corners, and that won't cut it in a court of law. We can't let emotion drive this investigation. Let us do our job. I'll talk to the county attorney this afternoon, but don't get your hopes up. Detective Willett is on your side. Let him do his job. We all feel for your loss, and we all miss Bill. And although I highly doubt that Doctor Malandra killed Bill, I'll be more than happy to see justice done if it's true. We'll see if we can find a way to do what you ask but do it by the book. One of us will give you a call this afternoon or tomorrow morning at the latest."

"Okay," Bryce said as he got up to leave. "Thanks for hearing me out at least."

By ten the following morning, Bryce still hadn't heard anything. He was still emotionally incapable of working and continued to have his staff shuffle appointments. He drove to police headquarters. "Nothing new?" he asked as he saw Willett coming down the hallway.

16

BRYCE CHECKED AT THE HOSPITAL TO MAKE SURE MALANDRA was not at work early Saturday morning, then followed Willett up the winding, gravel road to Malandra's property. Tony Malandra was stacking firewood but stopped short when he saw them pull into his driveway.

"Good morning, gentlemen. To what do I owe the honor? Oh! It's you, Bryce. I've been in New York, but I heard. I am so sorry for your loss."

"Thank you, Tony." It was all Bryce could do to force a smile.

"So, what's up?"

Willett took a step forward. "One of Doctor Thompson's patients ran away from home last night. He has diabetes and didn't take his insulin. No one knows if he had a destination, but he was last seen walking up this road. Have you seen anyone or anything out of the ordinary?"

"Not a thing, sorry."

"You don't mind if we look around, do you? This is a dead-end road, so this is the last place we have to look before we call for volunteers and start into the forest."

"By all means. Check it out. I'll help."

As Malandra turned toward the detached garage, Willett glanced at Bryce and gave him a nod. They searched the garage and found it empty. "That little storage shed is about the only other place someone could be hiding," Malandra said as he led them across the back property. It, too, was empty. "That's about it," he said.

"How about up on that hillside?" Bryce asked. "Didn't I see something up there?"

"Oh, that. That was where I was doing some taxidermy work, but there was a short in the old wiring, and when I smelled smoke, I had to tear it down. Nothing left but a pile of charred boards. Nowhere for a kid to hide, but you can check it out if you like, just to be sure. Beyond that, there's only forest."

Bryce and the detective hiked up the hill, leaving no stone unturned, and the shed was indeed demolished. They met Malandra at the bottom of the slope. "One last thing," Willett said. "Could we just take a peek inside your house, just in case he slipped in while you weren't looking? That's a common MO for runaways."

"Sure. That's a good idea. I've been outside this morning, and the doors have been unlocked," he said as he led them to the house.

Willett looked at Bryce and shrugged, a perplexed look on his face. "That was too easy," he whispered when they were several feet behind Malandra. Bryce returned the look, equally stunned.

They checked every room on the ground floor and then repeated the process on the second story. "Nothing here," Malandra said as they came down the stairs.

"How about the basement?" Willett asked. "That's where most kids try to hide."

"Of course. Follow me," he added as he led them to the stairwell. He turned on the lights and started down the stairs.

Bryce followed Willett, almost amused at what would happen when he exposed Malandra's secret. *He probably thinks he has that lab so well camouflaged that he has nothing to worry about. I can't wait to swing that false wall open and watch his smug grin disappear.*

"Not much down here," Malandra said as he swept an arm across the space. Those two side rooms are about the only places a kid could hide."

Not interested in the storerooms, Bryce stepped toward the back wall, then stopped short in mid stride. There, where the bookshelves had been, was a huge double-layered curtain of six-mil plastic hanging from the ceiling to the floor. The bookshelves had disappeared, the fume hood was gone, as were all the chemicals and beakers, and on the workbench under the exhaust fan was a brand-new wooden rocking chair with a fresh coat of polyurethane, the smell of fresh varnish unmistakable. "You son of a bitch. How ...?" But Bryce couldn't finish his sentence. He was too angry, too confused, and too perplexed to think clearly.

"It's a nice little workspace where I can do painting, varnishing, and taxidermy. The exhaust fan keeps the spray and fumes out of the rest of the house, and it never freezes, so I can use it year-round. Is there anything else you would like to see?" he asked as he turned toward Willett, smiling blandly.

"He's got to have cameras hidden around here. He knows I was here," Bryce whispered as he grabbed at the detective's sleeve and pulled him aside, pleading. "Requisition his computer drives, camera cards, whatever he uses for security. There will be all the evidence on those you need to believe I'm not crazy."

"We have no probable cause," Willett hissed.

"Hey, what am I missing out on here?" Malandra asked. "Are you okay, Bryce? Did you say security cameras?"

"I'm sorry, Doctor Malandra. Doctor Thompson has been under a lot of stress. He wants us to check your security system to see if the young man has been around here at all."

"No problem, Steve," Malandra interjected. "Have your IT guy come out and download the security system video. I've been out of town, so I'm sure all the movement you're going to see is sunrise and sunset shadows moving across the rooms."

"You've swept them clean, too, haven't you?" Bryce sputtered as he turned toward Malandra, his face reddening, the vein in his forehead bulging.

"Look, Bryce. I know you've been under intense stress, and I certainly hope you find your runaway patient, but I think you need to talk to Ulysses and get started on some medication. You need sleep and more time off." He turned to Willett. "I'll show you where the security camera hard drive is and give you the password. I can always reset it later." Upstairs, Malandra pointed out the security system and wrote down the password for Willett. "I need to go to the hospital. Look around all you want. Close the garage door when you leave, and make sure he gets some help," he added as he jerked a thumb toward Bryce. "PTSD is very real, and the suicide rate among doctors is at an all-time high. Let's get him some help," he added as he turned and headed for his car.

Willett pulled out his cell phone and dialed headquarters for IT as Bryce followed Malandra out through the garage. His rage was preventing him from formulating his thoughts and saying what he wanted to say. Malandra hopped into his car and backed out. As he started rolling forward, he lowered his window and smiled at Bryce, speaking quietly. "You know, I read in *Medical Economics* the other day that pathologists make twice as much as family docs. I guess it's because they're twice as smart," he added as he hit the gas and sped away.

Bryce Thompson stood alone in the driveway on the mountain-side and watched the taillights disappear as the car took the first curve and was out of sight. "I am an idiot!" he said aloud as he walked to his vehicle. "I should have gone straight to Willett in the first place. I contaminated the investigation because of my impatience," he mumbled as he got in and headed down the mountain. "No! I'm not an idiot. I am an absolute moron!"

17

HOURS TURNED INTO DAYS, AND NOTHING WAS HAPPENING IN the investigation. It was all Bryce could think about as he went over and over in his head how the deaths Bill was investigating could have been manipulated by someone who knew medicine and had access to the patients, particularly the ones who were hospitalized. A tiny detail missed before, it now dawned on him that all the hospital deaths had been late at night, when staffing was at a minimum and Malandra could more easily move about the halls of the hospital unnoticed. Additionally, the motorcycle could easily have been forced off the road by a banged-up pickup full of firewood that would be no worse for wear with a few more scratches on its right side, unnoticed and ignored in an already crumpled frame. How he had gotten to the last victim in his own home he couldn't tell, but once inside, it wouldn't be all that hard to spike a drink and then dust him off with the cocaine or whatever else he might have cooked up.

Monday morning, Bryce walked into the pathology department intending to confront Malandra and see how he handled the accusations, see how he would answer when alone with Bryce, see if he would incriminate himself. He had a digital recorder nestled in his jacket pocket, but entering the office area, he saw Malandra's office was dark. "Where is he?"

"I'm sorry, Doctor Thompson, but he had to return to New York. His mother took a turn for the worse, and he doesn't know how long it will be. He has taken an indefinite leave of absence."

"Thank you, Melanie," he said as he spun on a heel and left. "He's still one step ahead of me," he said to no one as he headed for home.

Back at his house, he retrieved the key that Bill had given him to his back door and drove across town. Bill's house was still considered a crime scene, although no officials had been there in days. He parked in the alley and walked across the uncut grass, unlocked the door, then carefully slipped between the yellow police tape criss-crossing the back door. Inside, he went directly to Bill's office and began going through the papers on the desk. Anything even remotely related to the insurance investigation he snapped pictures of, then put them back where he had found them. In the center drawer, he found a couple of pocket-sized notebooks that Bill always carried, and he put these in a bag.

The brothers had long ago shared the combinations to their home safes in case of emergency, and now he went to the little safe camouflaged as an end table, lifted the false cover, and opened the safe's door. A badge and passport, several pocket-sized notebooks, three pistols, and personal odds and ends were inside. He dropped the badge, passport, and notebooks into a bag. Nothing else in the safe referenced the investigation, so he locked it, then checked around the house for any other papers or notes that might have any relevance. Finding nothing of use, he slipped out, not disrupting the police tape.

Back at his house, he scrutinized every item, hoping for any clues. In one of the small notebooks, he struck gold. There, he recognized the names of the deceased from his medical record reviews, along with the addresses and phone numbers of the surviving spouses. Bill had jotted the amount of the cash settlement for each of the insured in the right margin. Bryce's next line of investigation was decided without a second thought.

18

UNABLE TO CONCENTRATE ON WORK, BRYCE INSTRUCTED HIS staff to reschedule appointments for the next month. Over the next few days, Bryce visited the surviving spouses he could locate, introducing himself as 'Detective Thompson' and flashing Bill's badge in their faces. He peppered them with questions, watching as they squirmed. Their body language spoke a different tongue than their mouths, but he could get nothing, not a hint, with his line of questioning. He had only been able to locate three of them, several having left town shortly after collecting the insurance money. The last one, Virginia Zebrowski, the most recently widowed multi-millionaire, had answered neither her phone nor her doorbell on four successive tries.

The morning dawn was reflecting pink and lavender under a diaphanous veil of cirrus as he parked a hundred feet down the block from her expensive three-story home. Bryce had packed elk jerky, cheese, crackers, water, and sodas and decided to wait until he saw activity, even if it took all day, or all week. As the pink sky gave way to the gold of the rising sun, he had his epiphany. Like the flash of sunlight in his eyes, it dawned on him that he had been going about his questioning all wrong.

I've been asking each in turn if they are guilty, and each in turn is denying it. I've been showing my hand. What if I approach this last one as if I know she is guilty? Not an accusation, not a conjecture, just an accepted fact? Take a lesson from Bill's playbook.

"Don't listen to their words," Bill had instructed, "watch their body language."

How will she react? Will she hesitate, fidget, or stammer? What do I have to lose?

An hour passed, then two, and finally the side door opened and a trim, attractive brunette stepped out and began watering potted plants, working her way to the back deck. Bryce stashed Bill's badge under the seat. No need for that today. He put on his sunglasses and pulled the baseball cap low over his eyes, hopped out of the car, and walked down the opposite sidewalk until he was past her house and out of view, then quickly crossed the street and rounded the house, approaching her from her own back yard, catching her off guard. "Good morning, Mrs. Z."

"Oh, God! You scared me," she said, eyeing her back door and edging toward it.

"Sorry, but I need some information."

"Information about what?"

"About my share of the insurance money. I did all the work, and he skipped town. Do you know how to contact him?"

"I have no clue what you are talking about," she whispered, breathless, taking a step toward her back door.

Bryce stepped between her and the door. "Look! I don't want trouble any more than you do, but I need that money. If I don't pay some debts, I'm a dead man. Either you tell me how to find him, or you pay me directly. Then I disappear. You'll never hear from me again."

"I don't know what you're talking about. Now, get off my property, or I'll call the police."

"I highly doubt that. The last thing you want is the police snooping around. One word from me and you'll be so embroiled in legal shit you won't know what hit you."

"Leave me alone! I have no idea what you're talking about, and I don't have to talk to you." She started toward the side door, but again Bryce cut off her retreat.

"Oh, I think you do have to talk to me. I either get information, or I get paid. Otherwise, I call the police and leave a trail that leads right to your doorstep. Is that where you want to go with this?"

She unconsciously wiped her brow, sun glistening on the beads of salty perspiration that had appeared despite the cool morning air. She rubbed her hands together repeatedly, as if the mere act of doing something would help her think. "I don't know anything about anything. We have nothing to talk about."

"Look, all I want is to get what's owed me. Have you already paid him?" He said it so earnestly, so confidently, that he left her no room to doubt that he knew what he was talking about.

"I don't know who 'he' is, whoever you're talking about. Now, leave!"

"Maybe just one anonymous phone call to the police station will jog your memory," he whispered as he retrieved his cell phone and began to punch in numbers.

"No! Don't," she blurted. It was pure reflex, but it spoke volumes.

"Okay. I'm listening." He cradled the phone, his finger dangling above the screen.

"Why do you think I should know what you are talking about?"

"Because I know your husband conveniently died of a drug overdose, died with cocaine spread all over the desk, died while you were in Paris with the perfect alibi, and left you a very wealthy lady."

The pink hues of her beautiful face drained to ashen at the accuracy of his statement, but she regained her composure after only a heartbeat. "People die every day. What's that got to do with me?"

"They don't usually die in their home office from a drug overdose, particularly someone not known to use drugs."

"How do you know any of this?" she stammered, her words forced.

"How do you think I knew where to find you? I've been here before, on a lonely Saturday evening when he was so conveniently home alone. When you were so conveniently out of town."

"What do you want?"

"Like I said. I did all the dirty work, and he took all the money. Now he's gone. He promised me ten thou. But now I'm pissed. I want more."

"How much more?"

"Fifteen would work. Small bills."

"Don't be ridiculous. I am going into my house now, and if you try to stop me, I will call the police."

"I'll give you a day to think about what I've said. I'll be back tomorrow morning, and if you try to leave town, I will know about it. You are being watched and don't even know it. If you get my cash, you will never hear from me again."

"I can't get cash that fast. Besides, how do I know you won't just keep coming back for more?"

"Some people keep their word. Unlike you. And him," he sneered. "I'll see you tomorrow at ten. You have my cash, or I'll have the police breathing down your neck." He turned abruptly and walked away.

Bryce negotiated a half-mile route around the expensive houses and manicured lawns before he circled back to his vehicle and slipped inside. He drove around a few minutes, then parked in a new spot, her house still in sight. He was not about to let her skip town on him now. Every few hours, he moved his vehicle, not wanting the neighbors to become suspicious of a strange vehicle in their exclusive neighborhood. Munching on jerky and sipping Pepsi, he watched the sun set in the west, and when the last lights went to sleep in the neighborhood, he drove his car home, showered and changed, then switched vehicles, repacking his pickup for the night's watch. Again, he parked far enough away to be inconspicuous, close enough to watch, and got comfortable for the night. His long years of training, his endless hours in the ER and ICU, now served him well. He wouldn't sleep, knowing this patient needed watching.

The sun rose brilliant and stark in a cloudless sky, and it was challenging his eyes as he watched for activity at her house. He had parked directly west of her house, and the sun was burning into his retinas. He couldn't see a thing. He started the vehicle and moved down the street. *Need more practice at this detective stuff. Bill would never have made that rookie mistake.*

Shortly after nine, a Mercedes Cabriolet pulled out of the garage. He followed from a hundred yards. She drove directly to the main branch of the First National and was inside barely five minutes before she scurried out and drove back to her house. Bryce parked at the far end of the street and watched for any activity, then, satisfied that she was alone, walked to the back deck and knocked on the door.

She opened the blinds and unlocked the sliding patio door, opening it only a few inches against a safety stop, no welcoming "come on in" gesture in her glare.

"Do you have what's owed me?"

"I could manage thirteen."

"Bullshit. You got millions."

"Banks have to report withdrawals over ten thousand."

"So, how did you pay him?"

"Electronic transfer to some bank account. No names. Just numbers. My bank just thought it was a savings transfer. He had it all set up. I don't know his name. I never saw his face. Only phone calls. I have no idea who he is. It was totally anonymous."

"But you couldn't miss that New York accent, could you?" Bryce went out on a limb with that assertion, but it could not have been more effective.

"I guess you do know him."

"Better than you care to know," he barely whispered. "So, I'm guessing it was his idea for you to be out of town, right?"

"Yes. That's all I know. I swear. Somehow, he knew we were having trouble. He knew my husband was screwing every bimbo he could get his hands on, as long as they were young. Brought me home a nice birthday present. Gonorrhea. That was the last straw."

"What did he tell you about the setup?"

"Nothing. He said the less I knew, the better. Just said my husband would get very ill very quickly. He said to get the most life insurance I could manage, and I would be well-rewarded with the estate and my half of the insurance money."

"If you didn't know him, why did he trust you to pay him?"

"That was the scary part. He said he knew I would pay up because he knew where I lived, but I didn't know where he lived. He said he could always find me and then I would really pay. Plus, he said I would never know when or how. I would always be looking over my shoulder, and that scared me more than anything. I wired the money the same day I got the check."

"How much did you get?"

"None of your business."

Bryce pulled a small spiral notebook from his pocket and opened it to a tagged page. "I would say five million if I had to guess." He looked her squarely in the eye as he folded the notebook in slow motion and slipped it back into his pocket.

An involuntary shudder coursed through her body as she reached into her purse. She pulled out a Crown Royal bag and tossed it to Bryce. "Here's the nine-nine from the bank plus the cash I had in the house. If you ever show up here again, I'll shoot you. Then I *will* call the police to report a thief breaking and entering." She closed and locked the door, then turned and disappeared into the house.

Bryce walked slowly to his truck, his reward not in a little purple bag but in the knowledge that Bill's instinct had been right all along.

19

"GOOD MORNING, DOCTOR THOMPSON," MELANIE SAID AS BRYCE walked into the pathology office.

"Hi, Melanie. Any word from Malandra? Does anyone know when he's coming back to work?"

"No, sir. He left a message that his mother had suffered another stroke. It sounds like it may be a while."

"Does anyone know where she lives?"

"Somewhere in New York is all I know. I guess he never said the name of the city."

"Melanie, I need a favor. Several weeks ago, there was a cocaine-related death on a William Zebrowski. Malandra did that autopsy. I reviewed his report. But I also checked the call schedule, and Jansen was on call that weekend. I was told Malandra was out of town, so how did he get the autopsy? Why didn't it go to Missoula? Be a dear, and check your calendar. See if there was a call switch that weekend."

She tapped into her keyboard for a few seconds, then replied, "You're right, Doctor Thompson. He was out of town for four days. Jansen was on call that weekend, but Tony flew in early Monday morning in his plane and was here when the body arrived. I remember now because Doctor Jansen was tired from a busy weekend and thanked him for taking the case. Saved him a ton of paperwork, the phone calls, the transfer, you know."

"Thanks, Mel. You're a gem."

Bryce walked to the stairwell and headed up to the administration offices. *Of course, he was out of town when Zebrowski died. His alibi is perfect. Then he magically appears early Monday morning and plays Mr. Nice Guy. He takes the autopsy, controls all aspects. Smart. Very smart.*

Knowing there was an executive staff meeting scheduled for noon, Bryce timed it to arrive at administration at ten minutes to twelve. "Good morning, Nancy. I hate to bother you, but I need to review my file. My malpractice insurance company is trying to raise my rates, and there have been no complaints or actions, so I need to send them some records."

Nancy looked at her watch and the pile of papers on her desk, a perplexed look of hesitation causing her lips to purse, forehead wrinkled. "I have to get to the boardroom. Can you come back at one?"

"I'm afraid not. I have a very sick patient at one."

She stepped to the file cabinets and quickly found his file.

"Thanks, Nancy. You don't mind if I make a couple of copies? I'll just leave the file on your desk when I leave."

"Okay. Be sure to lock the door on your way out. Sorry, I'm in such a hurry. You've been chief of staff. You know how these things work."

"Thanks. I'll lock up," he said as he began leafing through his file. The minute she scurried down the hallway, he closed and locked the door, then went back to the file cabinets and found Malandra's file. He secured the file cabinet, slipped the file into his back beltline under his jacket, dropped his own file on Nancy's desk, and locked the office door as he exited.

Back at the house, Bryce methodically went through Malandra's file until he found the original application for medical staff privileges. There, under "Notify in case of emergency," he found it. "Francis Malandra, 110 Elm Street, Hudson Falls, New York."

The following day, Bryce again visited the pathology department, querying Melanie, seeing if there had been any calls from Malandra—any updates on his plans for returning.

"Sorry, Doctor Thompson. Still nothing."

"Thanks, again. I'll stop pestering you. I just wanted to make sure there was nothing new," he said as he turned to leave.

He was mid-stride through the door when he saw a medical student studying the hanging skeleton of Eve in the middle of the lab area. He stared at the macabre grin of the skeleton, and like a bolt of lightning, Bill's voice was in his head like it was yesterday. *"Did you know he used to be married before he moved here? Married a Jill Downing from Waterford, New York. A little town of 8,000 in upstate between Albany and Saratoga."*

"You hear things. She died scuba diving, I guess."

"They were diving in South America when she disappeared. They never found the body, quit looking after several days, strong currents, coastal winds, assumed drowned and washed away. He collected over three million in life insurance."

Bryce froze as he stared at the bones, the hairs on his neck erect, the shudder involuntary. His mind raced back in time. *In the back of the shed was a large, glass-enclosed terrarium, and inside he could see the skull of a large black bear amid thousands of dermestid beetles. The skull was nearly devoid of flesh, the clean white bone shining in the dark interior.*

"Are you okay, Doctor Thompson?" Melanie's voice brought him back to the present.

"Sorry. I forgot something. It just dawned on me. Thanks. Call me if you hear from him."

Bryce returned long after dark, long after everyone had gone home except the on-call tech. He loitered in the stairwell until the tech took the elevator up to the medical floor for a blood draw. Slipping through the darkened department, he stepped up to Eve and tenderly opened her jaw. Bryce set the tension on the Vice Grip pliers to minimal so as not to crush a tooth, then, subconsciously, as if he didn't want to hurt her, very gently removed the back molars on each side of her lower jaw. It took a few minutes, being careful not to break the mandible, but he extracted them and secured them in a Ziploc. It would have been much easier to take a couple of phalanges from her fingers, but he knew that old, dried finger bones might not have enough marrow for the DNA testing he had planned. Bryce knew that the enamel protected the root of the tooth, and that was enough for identification in most cases. He exited as silently as he had entered and headed for home.

20

U TILIZING WHITEPAGES.COM, BRYCE WAS DISMAYED AT HOW many Downings lived in the Waterford, New York, area. His initial search revealed 229 listings, and what he thought would be a handful of phone calls now presented itself as a major task. However, reading more closely, he realized any listings even close to Waterford were included. Listings from Schenectady, Saratoga Springs, Mechanicville, even Albany, were tagged to the Waterford search, making the website thorough but daunting for what he wanted.

Pouring a steaming cup of coffee the next morning at six, he knew it would be eight in New York. People would be up. Calls would be answered. Beginning with Downing, Abby, he went through the A's, then the B's, then the C's, plodding through the alphabet and calling numbers within ten miles of Waterford, with dead end after dead end throughout the morning. Of those who did answer, no one knew of a Jill Downing or a Jill Malandra. It was late in the morning before he got to Downing, Melvin.

"Good morning, Mr. Downing. This is Detective Thompson from the Helena Police Department. I am looking for the family of

Jill Downing-Malandra, deceased. Would you have any information about her family?"

"Oh my God! I thought I would never hear those words. We assumed the police would never look back into her disappearance, despite our pleas. She was my niece. You'll want to talk to my brother, Tim. Timothy and Monica Downing. They live just a mile from here. Here are their numbers." He paused while Bryce jotted down the numbers. "Give me a minute. I'll let them know you'll be calling."

Bryce confirmed the numbers, heart palpitating at the news that this was not a waste of time after all. He waited ten minutes and dialed again.

"Good morning, Mr. Downing. This is Detective Thompson from the Helena Police Department. I have just been on the phone with your brother, Melvin, and he was kind enough to give me your number. I am looking into the disappearance of your daughter, Jill, in light of some new information that I have come across. May I ask you a few questions, sir?"

"Ask away, Detective. Ask away. I have you on speakerphone, and my wife is here with me. We had given up on ever getting this phone call, but you said Helena. Jill never lived in Helena. They were living in Billings when she disappeared. She had called us and told us she was going to leave that asshole, and the next thing you know they are supposedly scuba diving in the Pacific on a second honeymoon. What a crock. Monica and I flew out to Billings and tried to talk to their head detective, but he wouldn't take us seriously. Said every family grieves differently when they lose a loved one and tries to find an explanation when there is none. Said the good doctor was well-known and well-liked, even did some work for their department.

Wrote us off. I could see it if it hadn't been for that last phone call, but she had told us he was getting more and more weird on her, and she was getting out. Then she's gone, like a puff of smoke."

"Mr. Downing, do you happen to know how much life insurance he had on Jill?"

"No, I don't."

"We believe it was three million dollars."

"That fits with everything we know about Tony. Everything was all about money with him. I'll go to my grave convinced that he had something to do with her drowning."

"What if I told you I am not convinced that she drowned in South America?"

"Go on."

"I suspect that whoever went diving with him on that trip was not his wife but someone using her name and her passport. She could have been a paid accomplice, traveling under Jill's name to Ecuador, then disappearing and returning under her own name, leaving a paper trail of one Jill Downing-Malandra flying to South America but never getting her passport stamped coming back into the country. That way, no one is looking for a body in Montana."

"Jesus! How did you find this out?"

"It's merely conjecture so far, but I may have stumbled across some of her remains. I need DNA confirmation before I can do anything more. Do you have anything of hers that we can use to match a DNA analysis?"

"Nothing I know of. Monica?"

A sad, sweet voice came over the line. "No. There's nothing left of hers here."

"Could there be an old comb or hairbrush that would have her hair in it?"

"I can look, but I think everything in her bathroom got thrown out when we remodeled a couple of years ago."

"How about that first tooth fairy experience? Did you happen to save that in a baby book?"

"No. I'm sorry."

"A lock of hair, maybe." Bryce could feel things slipping away.

"No. Oh, my. I can't bear this. We're terrible parents," the voice trailed into tears, sobbing.

"How about old toys, something that could have hair entangled in it? Anything? Cut hair will not work. We would need the roots of the hairs for DNA analysis."

The pause was interminable, then Monica's voice recovered. "Tim! Her Barbies! Are they still in that tub? You know, in the west end of the basement?"

"Yes. I'm sure they are. I saw that tub a few months ago when I was looking for those Utah vacation pictures."

"She used to play Barbie makeup for hours. Those tiny brushes, she would do Barbie's hair, then her own. Maybe ..." her voice trailed off as footsteps clattered down a flight of stairs. Less than a minute passed before her voice came back on the line. "Here's that tub." Then random noises of plastic clicking on plastic before a triumphant voice said, "Here it is. That little pink brush. It has a lot of hair in it, some of Barbie's but a lot of her hair too. Will that work?"

"It might be perfect if her hair is the only hair in there. Could it be mixed with a friend's hair?"

"That's possible, but her best friend was a dark brunette. These are all blond. And if there are different colors, can't they separate those?"

"I'm sure they can. But if there are two blond types, we might have trouble proving which one is Jill's. Now, what I need you to do is to seal that in a heavy-duty baggie, date and sign it, and personally take it to a DNA lab. I have the name and address of one in Albany for you to use. Whatever you do, do not mail it. Not only could it get lost, but you must have control of it for what is called the chain of custody. I just overnighted them a sample, which they will give me a preliminary on, to make sure it is a female. If it is, then I will come to New York and bring my second sample. I can swear to its origin and have the same lab analyze and compare it to your hair samples. If there is a match, we might have him."

He gave them the name, address, and phone number of the lab in Albany. Bryce also explained why it was important to pay top dollar for the depth of accuracy required, not the ninety-nine-dollar specials on ancestry sites that give a ballpark but won't hold up in court. "If the data is consistent, I will be out there in a few days with my sample, then we can share information." He jotted down their address and bid them goodbye. For the first time in weeks, Bryce Thompson felt alive and energized again.

21

THE CASH FROM THE ZEBROWSKI WIDOW AND A FEW GENTLE withdrawals from his savings and business accounts stacked up on Bryce's kitchen table to a height of $22,000.00 and change. He packed one suit, one dress outfit, and comfortable casual clothes and jeans into his duffel. He threw the duffel into his newly purchased, slightly used, white Ford van that looked like any other work van in the country. He added a cooler with a variety of food and beverage choices, and just behind that he stashed his medical bag along with certain essential ingredients every ICU has in abundance. He strapped a sturdy cot to the left wall D-rings and placed the porta potty inside the back door. On the sides and rear door of the van, he attached his freshly-minted magnetic decals beaming the "Medical Transport Corporation" logo in bright fluorescent colors. Sometimes, the best camouflage is no camouflage.

The morning after he received the call from Albany confirming his tooth sample was from a female, the rising sun shone on a full thermos of coffee, a pack of cake donuts, fresh bananas, a pile of PB&J sandwiches, and a poorly-rested Bryce Thompson pulling onto the highway and pointing the van due east. Although tired, Bryce had every intention of keeping it pointed due east until he reached New York and the Hudson River Valley. On the console was a brand-new prepaid cell phone. His personal cell phone was powered off and locked securely in a ten-pound gun safe on the right-hand floor of the van. He was not about to have his phone ping him all the way to New York and back.

He slept a few hours here and there on the cot when his eyelids were too heavy to drive, and he stopped once for a good night's sleep and a long shower at a motel in eastern Ohio. Monday morning, three days later, found him pulling into the parking lot of the Albany DNA Forensics Laboratory.

Washing his face, neck, and trunk with baby wipes, he slipped on a fresh shirt, combed his hair, splashed some cologne on his neck, and walked into the front office. "Good morning," he said to the receptionist as he flashed Bill's badge. "I am Detective Thompson, and I have an appointment with your administrator, Mr. Carlyle."

"Of course, Detective, follow me," she said as she motioned him to a hallway leading to the labs in the back of the building. At the back of the hallway, she led him into a modest office that had wide picture windows on two walls, one looking out over the Hudson River and the other looking out over the laboratory where Carlyle could oversee the action in the lab. "Mr. Carlyle, this is Detective Thompson from Montana," the secretary said as she ushered Bryce into the office, then closed the door on her way out.

"Good morning, Detective Thompson. Welcome to Albany."

"Thank you, sir. Glad to be here," he added as he nonchalantly flashed Bill's badge and coolly slipped it back into his breast pocket as if he had been doing it all his life. He glanced around the room, taking in the diplomas and certificates gracing two of the walls. "I see you are a member of Azz-clad," he added, studying the framed certificate from the American Society of Crime Laboratory Directors.

"Absolutely. All forensics labs in the state are required to be accredited."

"And certified by state and federal boards?"

"Yes, sir."

"Were you ever affiliated with the Cybergenetics Company?"

"Absolutely not. I see you've done your homework. The state terminated its contract with Cybergenetics, and those caught cheating on the TrueAllele training exams were largely banned from practice in the state. I heard most of them left New York."

"Have you successfully incorporated STRmix?"

"We actually have one of the top researchers in the country working for us and have tweaked STRmix and developed something that we think is superior. You've probably read that STRmix had some criticism of its probabilistic genotyping software when it came to extreme sample mixtures. And since most crime scenes have a mixture of fluids, we don't often get clean samples, which you told me on the phone is what you are having us analyze."

"I sure hope so. I mailed you the lower left molar of a female skeleton, well-preserved. You confirmed that it was one hundred percent consistent with a human female. I have here the lower right molar from the same skeletal remains. These have been in my possession the entire time. The chain of custody is well documented. There could be insect dung contaminating it and human hand oils, like mine, from touching it."

"Not a problem. We'll surface clean it before we start."

"You met the Downings a few days ago?"

"Yes. Very nice couple. So sad."

"And their hair samples? Were they adequate?" Bryce added, a worried frown creasing his forehead.

"Yes. There were doll's hairs and human hairs in the brush, and all of the human hairs were blond except for one strand, which was dark brunette and easily separated. Under the microscope, the blond hairs all had uniform characteristics, so it doesn't look like a STRmix problem."

"You took the parents' statement that the brush was in their sole possession, sequestered in their home the past twenty-plus years, and no one could have tampered with it, correct?"

"Correct. We have their affidavit signed and notarized."

"If the hair samples give you any difficulty, would it be at all helpful to do a hair analysis on the mother to correlate genetics and authenticity?"

"Totally. That would simply add a million-to-one guarantee that it was her daughter, although if the hairs match the tooth, and the hairs were always in their possession, that is usually enough to convict."

Bryce gazed out over the river valley, then turned back to Carlyle with a hopeful look. "So, what is our timeline to a full analysis?"

"Well, as I'm sure you are aware, Detective, crime labs across the country are terribly backlogged and the press is crying for action on thousands of cold cases. There have just been too many innocent men, mostly black men, sitting in jails, awaiting justice. We are no exception. It will take a while to get your samples into the work queue. I'm sorry."

"That does not work for me. You are the director here. Don't you set priorities?"

"Of course, but although we are privately owned, we have contracts with the state, and they are breathing down my neck constantly about their timelines. Everyone has timelines." He shrugged his shoulders and held out his palms. "And everyone thinks theirs is the most important."

"Cold cases are cold for a reason, but I have every reason to believe this perp knows we're on to him and will leave the country if there is any delay. That just can't happen, Mr. Carlyle. I am paying in cash, and I am willing to pay priority fees if necessary. Perhaps I can buy the staff some pizza." Bryce pulled out a small roll of hundred-dollar bills, then slowly, tantalizingly, pulled off the top bill. "Or a catered dinner," he added as he pulled the second bill from the roll so slowly Carlyle could hear the paper crinkle.

"Detective, I know you have a job to do, and I can tell you are passionate about your mission, but you have to realize that my staff is already working long hours, and the unions are very strict here about work-week hours." He was talking to Bryce but looking now at the third hundred-dollar bill uncurling from the roll.

"Surely, there must be some way we can make that clock tick a little faster?" Bryce added as the fourth bill came off the roll.

"Perhaps."

"Such as?" Bryce asked.

"Perhaps a sample could be moved to the front of the docket." Carlyle swallowed.

"Or two samples concurrently?" Bryce added as he pulled off the fifth bill. "Like, tomorrow morning?" he asked as he unfurled the sixth and final bill.

"I'm sure something this important can easily be prioritized," Carlyle said as Bryce shook his hand, the bills resting comfortably in Carlyle's handshake.

"You've been most helpful. I'll pay the front office in cash. You've been such a help, and I'm sorry to be a bother, but ..." Bryce let the statement hang, the unspoken words saying it all.

Bryce gave Carlyle the number to the no-contract phone he had purchased for anonymity. "Call any time, day or night, with any questions, and call the minute you have results." He thanked him again, paid the analysis fees, then walked, elated but wary, to his van and headed north. The sun was dull and weak through gray clouds and smog when he pulled into the driveway of Tim and Monica Downing's home that evening.

22

ALERTED BY HIS PHONE CALL, THE DOWNINGS WERE STANDING on the landing of the three-step entryway to their modest frame house, the looks on their faces as sad as the evening sky. Jill had been their only child, and looking at their forlorn countenance, Bryce could almost see the scar of their loss carved across their faces.

"Good evening, Detective Thompson," Mrs. Downing said as she came down the steps in front of her husband, taking Bryce's hand in a warm, prolonged handshake. "It is so nice to meet you. We can never thank you enough for taking this case seriously. I have a prime chuck roast ready to slice, and potatoes, gravy, and sweet peas. I insist that you stay with us tonight. You must be exhausted from that drive."

"You shouldn't have gone through all that trouble, but I have to admit a real meal after three days of coffee and donuts does sound awesome."

"Welcome," Tim Downing said as he took Bryce's hand in a powerful grip. "Can I interest you in a glass of wine?"

"I can't turn that down after all these days on the road," Bryce answered as he followed them into the living room.

"I opened a syrah. Is that okay?"

"Perfect," Bryce replied as he looked around the room, unable to miss the large, high school graduation portrait on the wall above the mantel. "So, this must be Jill," he said, his eyes riveted on the beautiful face.

"Yes. My baby." Monica's voice broke slightly, the long-subdued hurt rekindled with this new entry into their lives. "I guess she'll always be my baby."

"We meet at last," he said quietly to the ghost on the wall, pleased to replace the stark grin of the skeleton in the pathology department with the stunning face looking down on him now.

They made acquaintance conversation during their repast, getting to know each other a little on the personal level, Bryce mostly asking questions and avoiding the facts of his real life. The fact that he was now Detective Thompson was not a lie; he was doing exactly what Bill Thompson would be doing.

"That was amazing," he said as he finished the last of his beef. "I don't remember when I had a roast that was that tender and juicy."

"It has to be done low and slow," Monica said, the proud grin adding life to her countenance. "Most people are impatient and hurry it; too fast and too hot, and the meat toughens and dries. And always add a cup or two of water to the bottom of the pan. It keeps it moist, and your gravy is ready to thicken."

"Well, you have me convinced," he added as he began to clear his dishes.

"No. Leave them. I insist. You haven't come two thousand miles to do dishes. Let's sit and talk."

"Another glass of syrah?" Tim asked. "Or would you like a pour of Baileys Irish Cream?"

"Now that does sound good. I haven't had Baileys in ages."

Tim poured their after-dinner drinks, and they retired to the front room.

"So, tell me about Tony and Jill. I need some backstory to fill in the blanks. Of course, all of this depends on whether or not my assumptions are correct. If my sample matches the hair samples, there can't be a one in a million chance that the court will call it circumstantial. But we won't know for several days."

"How psychotic can you be? I literally got sick at the thought of my daughter's remains hanging there for all to see and examine. Your own wife's bones? I just can't imagine it."

"I thought it was a long shot at first. But the size and sex were such that I had to look into it. After you told me that Jill was five-four, thin-hipped, and had broken her collarbone, that was the clincher. The slight deformity in the left clavicle is there if you know what to look for. So often, it is one little clue that can make or break a case."

"But why would he keep her bones?"

"You can't ask psychiatric patients logical questions and expect logical answers. Their logic is theirs alone. What I can tell you is that Tony Malandra is a collector. He collects cars. That isn't strange in itself. Most guys would love to do the same if they could afford it, but he also collects trophies. I've been in his house. He has multiple mounts from his African safaris, North American grizzly and black bear mounts, Dall sheep, bighorn and Stone sheep, elk, moose, and mountain lion. Again, that in itself is not strange. There are thousands of guys who would love to be able to afford those high-dollar hunts. A hunter is proud of the skill, strength, and patience it takes to stalk a big game animal, particularly a dangerous one like a lion or a bear. And it's natural to brag about it, show other alpha males that you are the top predator, the apex of the evolutionary chain. But when you put his strange behavior together with all of that, and the fact that we are investigating his possible involvement in six or seven other deaths, maybe more, a different profile emerges."

"Eight," Tim whispered, his Baileys wholly forgotten.

"So. Tell me about Tony and Jill. When did they meet? Where did they meet? What is their story?"

"They met in community college in Albany," Monica began. "Tony was the top of his class but couldn't afford the Ivy League schools. His father had a dry-cleaning business but died young, so Tony had to work his way through school. He and Jill hit it off right away, and she got her two-year associate's degree in accounting. She had planned to transfer to a four-year program, but that was when Tony proposed, and he went on to finish his pre-medical work. She worked full time to help put him through medical school. He was getting some good scholarships by then, and everything was looking like a dream come true. We thought she had the perfect life all set up when he started getting different."

"Take your time," Bryce interjected softly when she paused to catch the tears on her cheeks.

"It was toward the end of his pathology residency. We only learned this later. Too late, as it turned out. He started hurting her, just a little bit at first, if she did anything wrong. The first time was when she burned their supper, and he flew off the handle, hitting her. Then he said he was sorry and apologized profusely. As in so many abusive relationships, she just kept trying harder, thinking that if she could just do things a little better, the violence would stop. Oh, God. If I had known any of this at the time, I would have told her to get out. But she hadn't confided in me until she worked up the nerve and made the decision to leave him. That conversation still haunts me. It was the way she told it that made me shudder. She said that as time went on and the pattern repeated itself, she realized that hitting her turned him on, and he needed to have sex right then while she was still crying. When she would try to have 'cuddly love,' as she called it, he was lackluster." Monica paused and took a sip of her drink. "It's strange talking about your little girl's sex life. I feel so guilty for not figuring it out until too late. Not doing anything. I should have sensed what was going on. I'm her mother, for crying out loud, but I failed her."

"You couldn't have known, Monica. You were thousands of miles away. You can't carry that burden. No one can know what goes on in that kind of marriage. In that kind of mind."

"I didn't know much about partner violence back then, but you can bet I've read a lot since. It's classic in retrospect. Anger, violence, remorse, then expensive gifts to buy back her love, assuage his guilt."

"At least she tried to share that much with you, tried to get out."

"Yes. Too little, too late. She had flown out here for a week for Tim's surprise birthday party. I'll never forget that week. That's when I made her tell me what was going on. She would spend an hour in the bathtub in the morning and an hour before bedtime. She was walking funny. A mother knows, you know? Anyway, I was doing some laundry when I found blood on her panties. Not in the front of her panties. In the back. Believe me, a woman knows blood on panties. So, I waited until Tim went to bed, then I sat her down after a few glasses of wine and made her talk. In vino veritas, you know."

"Oh, yes. I know."

"It was after that week that we encouraged her to get out. We should have done it differently, but you don't really know until after the fact. We should have insisted that she make a clean break and come live with us, get that separation, but we let her do it her way. She felt like she owed it to him to explain things, try to reason with him. And as always, he apologized and pleaded and cried for forgiveness. Whenever he cried, she melted, kind soul that she was. Then the next thing you know, their anniversary was coming up, and he has this trip to South America lined up. She had always wanted to see the Galápagos Islands before they were ruined, so he had the perfect carrot out on a stick. And you know the rest." She caught a falling tear as Tim got up and poured Bryce another Baileys.

Tim had been still most of the evening, the strong, quiet type who let his actions speak instead of his words. He poured out the creamy liqueur, then raised his glass to Bryce. "I shouldn't say this out loud, especially in front of a cop, but if you guys don't get him, and he *is* back here in New York, well, accidents happen." Then he raised his glass to Jill's picture and drank. No tears from the Tim

Downings of this world, just pinpoint pupils in a furrowed stare and a set jaw that meant business.

"Don't worry, Mr. Downing. If those samples match, we'll have him."

The following morning found Bryce up and showered and ready to depart almost before the Downings were out of bed. Monica was hastily making coffee and begging him to stay for one last, home-cooked meal, while Bryce was impatient to head north. Hudson Falls was calling. "Thank you so much for your hospitality," he said as he filled his mug with steaming coffee, "but I have too much to do to stay any longer." He gave Monica a hug and Tim an extra-long hand-shake. "I'll call as soon as I have information," he said as he held Tim's grip, a bond there unspoken.

They followed him to his van to say a last goodbye, the only observer the rising sun watching like a single yellow eye peaking over the horizon from somewhere above the Atlantic. "I need one more hug," Monica said as she enveloped him in her arms. "Thank you so much. I feel like I've known you for years. You feel like family somehow. Thank you so much for trying. For us. For Jill."

"Goodbye," Bryce said, "and thank you for everything. Knowing Jill a little might help me with perspective. Some day, I hope we'll know the whole story. Some day, maybe I'll make it back here, and we can have closure. You have my number if anything new comes up." He bid them farewell, started the van, and pulled out toward Highway 4 north. He waved out the window as the Downings receded in his rearview mirror. *Maybe then I can tell you the whole story. Maybe then you'll know why we feel like family. We are all that's left in Tony Malandra's wake.*

23

BRYCE KEPT THE RISING SUN OFF HIS RIGHT SHOULDER, THE VAN paralleling the Hudson River north, and soon traversed Mechanicville and was coursing below the bluffs of Saratoga National Historical Park on his left, the river on his right. It was a destination he and Nicole had discussed visiting some day, doing a deep dive into the Revolutionary War, and touring the famous battle-field where the dramatic victory over the British changed the course of the revolution. But for now, he had his own war to deal with.

Crossing the river north of Schuylerville at the junction of 4 and 32, Fort Miller and Fort Edward were soon behind him, the river now on his left. Minutes later, he could see the huge bend in the river to the west and the village of Hudson Falls ahead. Entering the city limits where Highway 4 widens into Main Street, careful not to exceed the speed limit, Bryce cruised around the old town. Like a new honeybee just out of the hive, he got his bearings circling Elm Street in wider and wider circles until he knew his environment. He noted the Walgreens in the center of town. *Always good to know where to find medical supplies.*

He found the little ice cream parlor north of the park and figured out the obtuse backtracking needed to get to Bridge Street in case of a hurried exit across the Hudson to the west. The auto parts store on the corner of Elm and Main was an easy-to-spot landmark for the entrance to his destination on Elm Street. Finally, his bearings well imprinted, he turned down Elm Street and cruised its length, dashcam rolling, then exited the far end of the street and turned north.

Returning to the ice cream parlor, he ordered a sandwich and a strawberry shake and then retreated to his van. He replayed the dashcam video of 110 Elm Street, the quiet, white, plain two-story house with the teak Cambridge rockers on the covered porch. Although he had surveyed the aerial view of the residence on the Internet, the dashcam provided the detail he needed.

The attached garage was early twentieth-century design, single stalls common when most families had but one car. A small storage shed in the back of the oversized, water-starved yard rounded out the property. Bryce studied the films over and over, making certain he had memorized the layout, covered every angle, then finished his lunch and drove to the self-service car wash. There he refueled and washed down the van. Making certain no one could see inside the drive-through stall, he swapped out the "Medical Transport Corporation" decals for the "Hudson Valley Power Company" magnetic decals. Satisfied, he drove back to Elm Street and parked down the block in front of a yard that had not been mowed in weeks and whose front gate was hosting a two-foot honeysuckle. He parked so he had a good view of Francis Malandra's front door and settled in to wait. How long he might have to wait, Bryce had no inkling. Tony

123

Malandra might not even be in New York, but he had no other clues, nowhere else to start.

When he purchased the van, Bryce made sure it had darkly tinted windows to deter prying eyes. Settling comfortably into the bucket seat, he picked up his Zeiss Conquest 10 x 56 binoculars, a steal at $1,500.00, and studied the house further, window by window. It was now midday, and there was sunlight bathing the house, reflecting off the glass and giving him little opportunity to peer inside. He watched for nearly half an hour before he saw movement inside the front window. Was it a man's shadow or that of an elderly widow? The shadow looked no taller than mid-window height, maybe five foot three inches at most, not Tony Malandra's five-foot-ten frame. He waited. An occasional shadow passed a window here and there over the next two hours. It wasn't until hour four that he confirmed two shadows together behind the front window, one silhouette several inches taller than the other.

"Bingo! Who else would be in there? Welcome home, loving son."

He waited. Whatever they were doing in that house, it was sedentary. Very little movement was appreciated for the next five hours, and Bryce decided it was time to move the van to reduce suspicion and to get some food. He drove to the Burger Shack and ordered a double cheese and fries, then drove into the alley behind the vacant house. He parked with just enough of the van's back window exposed to allow himself a direct line of vision to 110 Elm Street.

Sitting on a folding campstool, he could easily spot from his rear window with little chance of being seen from across the way. He waited. As darkness slowly insinuated itself into the river valley this

124

long summer day, and lights slowly came on around the village, the optics were reversed. Looking from bright sunlight into darkened windows, little can be seen, but looking from darkness into light, the retina is awash with contrasting photons. With the superb Zeiss optics, he could now see activity. Every curtain in the house was drawn, those inside welcoming no peering eyes. However, four windows on the main floor had sheers, revealing silhouettes. There were definitely two people inside, one short, shoulder-length hair, bent, shuffling, the other taller, short-cropped, straight, quick.

He waited. Dusk became full dark and still no hint was offered to confirm identification. Ten o'clock became eleven, and now only one shadow could be seen moving about as light after light was turned off inside. Eleven turned into midnight, and Bryce's eyes were starting to ache. Finally, the last light in the back corner of the house went dark, all activity ceased, and Bryce fired the engine and retreated for the night. He drove to the campground north of town and checked in, paying in cash and signing "Tim Downing" on the bottom of the ticket. He was not about to leave his name anywhere in New York if he could help it.

Five hours of fatigued sleep found Bryce awake and feeling the need for motion this Wednesday morning. He cleaned up quickly in the cold and moldy brick stall the campground had labeled "Men's Shower" but looked more like an outdated car wash and was soon on his way back to Elm Street, stopping long enough to grab an oversized coffee. Picking a different area to park further down the street, he grabbed a pack of mini donuts and sat back and waited.

And waited. The sun rose gently behind him, not glaring into his eyes. He had learned that lesson. Most of the day was like that;

Bryce sitting and waiting, the house sitting and aging. Daylight turned into midday, and there was still no activity outside the walls. Afternoon turned into evening, evening turned into dusk, the lights came on and went out, and he knew nothing more than he had the night before.

Back at the campground, he changed into jogging gear and walked around the perimeter of the grounds, stretching out the cramped muscles that had sat in the cramped van for too many hours for too many days. After he stretched and limbered up, he broke into a jog and clocked the perimeter a second time at a respectable pace, then again at a six-minute mile pace. Refreshed, he showered and returned to his van, the cot inviting after the long day. The run had done him good, and he slept the dreamless sleep of the innocent.

Back at Elm Street before dawn, he picked yet a different parking spot. And waited. Day three passed as had the day before, with no activity other than the occasional shadows gliding by the picture window.

Friday was passing just as monotonously, when, early in the afternoon, his phone rang. Caller ID showed "Carlyle/Forensics." He answered immediately, hoping and fearing in one blended, confused emotion.

"Thompson here."

"Hello, Detective Thompson. I have your results."

"And?" Bryce asked, the staccato response betraying his impatience.

"Your tooth is a perfect match with the hair samples the Downings brought in."

Relief washed over Bryce like a cool breeze on a July day. He hadn't wasted his time. "Excellent! I can't thank you enough."

"You already thanked me," Carlyle said. "Legally, I can't talk to the Downings about this aspect of your investigation without your permission. How do you want to handle this?"

"I'll call them. You just be sure you have everything documented, every 'T' crossed and every 'I' dotted. When this goes before a judge, I don't want some technical snafu."

"Don't you worry, Detective. That is the essence of our job description."

"I'm traveling right now, so I can't accept a package, but when I get back to Montana, I will call you with an address, and you can overnight the documentation. Thank you again."

"My pleasure. I'll wait to hear from you."

Bryce's pulse was racing as he signed off. Now, he had the information he needed to justify his plan. Now, his waiting didn't seem like waiting.

The rest of the day replayed like a rerun of the last three, and before he knew it, his watch was closing on 10 p.m. again. The lights at 110 Elm Street had been extinguished room by room, now only one faintly glowing in the back corner of the house like the night before. Just as Bryce decided to pack up his gear, the garage light flashed on, and the single garage door slowly opened, bathing the driveway in a dull glow from within. A dark, four-door sedan backed out and started down Elm toward Main. Bryce started his van and followed. There was little traffic, so he kept his distance. When the sedan pulled into the parking lot of the Hannaford Supermarket,

Bryce pulled to the curb and grabbed his binoculars. In the dull lights of the parking lot, the precision optics now paid their dues.

"Hello, Doctor Malandra. Long time no see." Saying it out loud made it seem more real somehow. "How would you like an all-expenses-paid trip to Montana?"

He repositioned his van and waited until Malandra came out carrying two grocery bags, then followed even more distantly, watching until the musty Oldsmobile pulled into the garage and was sealed in by the closing door. *You can't stay inside forever.* He drove back to the campground and had his first true slumber in weeks.

24

PREDAWN SATURDAY WAS ABUSTLE AT THE CAMPGROUND. BRYCE boiled water for instant coffee, grabbed a quick shower, then drove to the back yard of the unoccupied house. He waited. All day and little activity. He was beginning to think step two of his plan would never happen, but then, around 6 p.m., the garage door opened, and the rusting Oldsmobile backed out. There were now two people in the car, and he followed at a discrete distance. When the Olds pulled into a local steak house, Bryce stopped across the street and rolled down his window. He could hear Malandra's upraised voice carry across the pavement as he helped the old lady out of the car. *Good. She's hard of hearing. One less thing.*

With the doting son treating his mother to dinner, Bryce had at least an hour to reconnoiter. He pulled away and headed for Elm Street.

His makeover took a mere three minutes, and soon a shuffling, bent, gray-bearded man listing on a cane, baseball cap dangling a gray ponytail, was ambling toward the house at 110. He bypassed the front door and the walk-in garage door, trundling instead to the back of the house where the rear exit was largely hidden from peering eyes. A quick check confirmed it was locked, and Bryce deftly pulled the 15-inch pry bar from under his jacket. Wedging the flat end into the doorjamb, he loosened the jamb enough to fit the pry bar between the frame and the door. A quick thrust moved the aging wood enough to push the door beyond its locks. A few taps of the curved end of his Wonder Bar reseated the jamb, and only close inspection would reveal scratches in the peeling paint.

Inside, Bryce retrieved the compact Sony 35 mm camera and switched to 4K digital video recording. He immediately began filming every wall of every room using the built-in image stabilization feature. Careful to check for hidden security cameras inside the house, he went room to room, finding things of little interest in the old widow's den. Typical kitchen and dining areas led into a front room straight out of the 1950s, with yellowed pictures hung perfectly straight on yellowed wallpaper above faded, flowered furniture. A cramped back room next to the garage exit was being used as an office, with an oak desk and matching filing cabinet taking up most of the space. A huge, antiquated safe with faded lettering proclaiming Malandra Dry Cleaning stood against the inner wall. As he filmed each wall, Bryce noticed a fresh piece of white paper tacked to the wall next to the safe. There was a strange poem typed on it. He did a quick close-up of it. Everything about the place was old and yellowed; this was crisp, new, and avant-garde. He paused a moment to read.

Xerxes in the cataracts,
opium in the pill.
Sad go the decades,
in which we all fall ill.
Deceased, forlorn cadaver.

Strange. But then, Malandra probably wrote it. Why wouldn't his poetry hint of Poe?

He scanned the camera across the papers on the desk, careful not to disturb anything. He snapped close-ups of each paper for later review, but nothing looked remarkable. Behind the desk chair in the corner of the room against the outside walls, a small closet held a few winter coats and sweaters.

Upstairs revealed nothing of interest. A typical three-bedroom layout, two for sleeping and one for sewing and storage, and a small-ish bathroom with a claw-foot tub but no shower bespoke the era of the architecture. A storage closet at the end of the hallway rounded out the upper story layout. Nothing up there lent itself to Bryce's needs. Retreating to the first floor, he went back to the room with the desk and the antique safe and unlocked the single window, testing its travel. Significant sticking and squeaking revealed little use. Having thought this through a dozen times during the past days, Bryce was prepared. He retrieved a piece of paraffin from his pocket and vigorously coated the upper half of the jambs with wax, then forced the window fully open. Rubbing the wax vigorously up and down inside the lower jambs eventually allowed free and quiet travel. He unhooked the interior locks on the old-style screen and made sure it swung free on its hangers. He closed the window, leaving it unlocked, and vacated the property.

Returning to the van, he settled in and waited. An hour later, the Oldsmobile pulled into the garage, and the evening played out like the previous nights, with lights slowly extinguishing until only one remained in the back office of 110 Elm Street. Around midnight, that last light went out. The pattern had been fairly consistent—lights out near midnight, lights on around 7 a.m.

Bryce returned to the campground and readied everything he would need for the morning, then shed the disguise and showered. Making sure he had everything he needed in his small backpack, he slept, fitfully at best, and was up by four. Parking down the block, he walked rapidly to the back of 110, lifted the screen off its hangers, and set it silently against the house. He raised the window without a squeak, listened for movement for a minute, then set his pack inside the little room and crawled ever so slowly and soundlessly inside the house. He closed the window and retrieved what he needed from the backpack, then opened the closet door, stepped inside, pulled the door nearly closed, and waited. Through the crack of the door, he could just see the chair in front of the computer on the desk, and he hoped it would not be all day before Malandra came to the office to get online.

The next two hours passed agonizingly. First total quiet, then rustling upstairs and water running, a toilet flushing, doors opening and closing, footsteps descending, water running in the kitchen, a stove knob clicking, gas hissing, a puff of ignition, water boiling, aromas of coffee reaching his nostrils. Finally, after what seemed like hours, Tony Malandra sauntered into the little office, mug in hand, and took a seat in front of the computer. As he logged on, Bryce opened the closet door, took a single step, and collared Malandra with a three-foot piece of rope before Malandra even realized there was movement behind him.

"Move one muscle, and you're a dead man," he whispered as he tightened the garrote. "If you want to live, you will do exactly as I say."

Malandra jerked to his left, elbowed Bryce in the side, tried to rise and struggle free, but Bryce's six-foot-four, 220-pound frame easily overcame the 175-pound man with a rope around his neck, his air supply already noticeably restricted.

"Sit still, or I'll tighten it further," he whispered in Malandra's ear as he applied more pressure to the cord. As he felt Malandra's resistance soften, he grasped both ends of the cord with his left hand, pulled a syringe from his pocket, popped the cap off with his teeth, and plunged the needle into Malandra's trapezius muscle, where the neck muscles meet the shoulder. Malandra surged at the pain, pulling away from Bryce's one-hand hold, but Bryce had the plunger fully seated in less than a second. Malandra lunged back and gained his feet, his strength amplified with the rush of adrenalin. He tried to head snap the back of his skull into Bryce's face, but he was too short, and the move failed. He stomped on Bryce's left foot with all the force he could muster, and Bryce could feel his grip weakening on the cord until he got both hands back on the ends, then flipped Malandra onto his back and held him still with his entire weight crushing the air out of Malandra's lungs.

"One last time, give in, or I will have no choice but to strangle you."

Malandra couldn't talk, his airway too compromised, and Bryce could feel his muscles yielding. He held him in that position until the Haldol and Valium took over. Normally given in one or two milligram doses, the twenty that Bryce injected had Malandra sound asleep in a few minutes.

Bryce tidied up the evidence of the scuffle, closed the closet door, rehung the screen and locked the window, then walked to the stairwell and made certain there was no sound from the second floor. The elderly widow, nearly deaf, was still snoring, oblivious. Bryce went out through the garage and brought the van around, backing up to the garage door. As quietly as possible, he hoisted Malandra across his shoulder in a fireman's carry, carried him to the back of the van, and laid him out on the cot. He closed the garage door, started the van, and began the long road back to justice.

25

WITH A FULL TANK OF GAS AND PLENTY OF FOOD AND DRINK, Bryce's chief concern now was to avoid an accident or a speeding ticket. Outside of town, he pulled off onto a side road and replaced the power company's magnetic decals with the medical transport set. Next, he changed into his surgical scrubs and hung his stethoscope around his neck. If he was stopped for any reason, his cover was as good as he could make it, complete with his Montana Medical ID and his AMA card. He turned into the southbound lanes of early morning traffic and slipped between two eighteen wheelers driving just under the speed limit in the right lane. He angled southwest to intercept I-87. From there, he would blend into the anonymity of the I-90 system toward Buffalo. The I-90 would take him south of the Great Lakes and Chicago, into the sweeping plains of the Midwest, and eventually home.

Once he was on I-87, he pulled off into the first rest area, parking in the far corner. Malandra was still sound asleep, but there was no guarantee how long that would last; different people metabolize drugs at different rates. Bryce stripped him down and put on a double Attends diaper, hospital pajama pants, and an open-back hospital gown with snap-up arms for IV access. He quickly started an IV with a slow drip of five percent dextrose in normal saline, then piggy-backed a small bottle of Valium into the IV line using a battery-powered pump to ensure continuous dosing. He set the pump at a high adult dose to keep Malandra asleep but still breathing, placed an oxygen sensor on his finger, and strapped both arms and both legs to the cot with plastic ties to prevent him from getting up or yanking his IV should the Valium wear off while in heavy traffic. Between the seats, he had the backup syringe ready for a STAT dose should that happen.

Back on the freeway, he drove steadily and was into Ohio in no time. He refueled and relieved himself at roadside stops, and by the time the sun was glaring into his eyes above the burnt-orange horizon, he was west of Chicago and into open country. Although his adrenaline had carried him through almost four states, the pace of the last week was finally taking its toll. Sleep deprived and driving into the reddening sun, his eyelids felt like lead weights. He needed sleep to avoid an accident, and it seemed like forever before he found another rest area in Wisconsin. He pulled into the far corner again, made sure that Malandra was asleep and his IV bag was full, then rolled a sleeping bag out on the floor next to the cot and was soon asleep.

26

UNCERTAIN IF IT WAS THE TAPPING ON THE WINDOW OR THE glare of the flashlight that awakened him, Bryce bolted up in his sleeping bag, frantically searching for the zipper pull. By the time he freed himself, he was in total disarray, mind racing, heart pounding. It took a second before he realized there was a highway patrol officer standing outside his van, the leash of his canine partner in one hand, a flashlight in the other. Bryce slipped into the driver's seat, rolling down the window as he carefully repositioned his stethoscope for the trooper to see. "Hello, Officer. May I help you?"

"Sorry to bother you, sir, but we have a credible report of a male suspect driving a light-colored van who is soliciting truck drivers. We believe there is probable human trafficking at issue. May I see your license and registration?"

"Of course," he stammered as he reached for his billfold and withdrew his driver's license, then took the registration from the glove box. Even though he had worked up a line for a potential traffic stop, his heart was racing faster than it had after any 800-meter competition. He shook his head and rubbed his eyes, trying to gain composure. He glanced at his watch. It was 5 a.m.

"This looks in order," the officer said as he handed the cards back to Bryce. "Do you have a problem with me looking inside your van, sir? I do not have a search warrant, but if you volunteer access, it would speed up my job. It will only take a minute for Churchill here to clear your interior."

Bryce's palms were so wet he had to wipe them on his knees and his mouth so dry his tongue stuck to his palate. "OK, but be extra quiet. I am a doctor, and I have a patient in back who is sleeping, and we can't afford to wake him," he explained as he pulled his AMA card and his FDA registration card from his wallet. He handed them to the officer while he explained as naturally as if he did this every day. "He is suffering from alcohol withdrawal seizures and cannot tolerate any stimulation. Have you ever seen full-blown DTs?"

"No, only in training films."

"Well, it isn't pretty. He just got over the DTs yesterday and is sedated now. So, please, very, very slow and quiet, OK?"

"Of course, Doctor," he replied as he handed back the cards.

Bryce slipped between the seats, and while the officer led his dog around to the far side, Bryce quickly snipped the plastic tie from Malandra's right wrist, the left hidden near the far wall under the blankets. He unlocked the sliding door and very slowly slid it open, his finger to his lips in the universal sign for quiet.

The English springer spaniel stepped gingerly into the van, well-trained and disciplined as all police dogs must be to graduate into service, and he quietly sniffed the interior, stopping only at the edge of the cot to double-check the IV tubing coursing into the back of the human's hand. Bryce slid his medical bag to the edge of the door so the officer could peer inside.

"Why isn't he being transported by ambulance?" the patrolman asked, always suspicious.

"No money." Bryce's answer was quick and matter-of-fact. "He's my half-brother. I'm doing this for my mother. He's pissed away all his money and was slowly rotting on the streets in New York. At least in Montana, we can get him set up with a cheap apartment and a job, that is, if he'll stay sober and show up for work."

The dog had returned to his master's side and was quiet and relaxed. His demeanor made a statement. Reflexively, the officer relaxed as well. "I had a cousin who did the same thing. Broke his mother's heart."

"Amen to that," Bryce said. "Addicts think only of themselves, oblivious to their family's torment as they are forced to watch them perform their slow-motion suicide." He put the medical bag back next to the head of the cot and stepped out of the van, stretching. "You wouldn't happen to know if 90 through South Dakota or 94 through North Dakota would be the better route for construction and delays, would you? It's about the same distance either way." Nonchalant small talk changed not only the subject but also the tenor of the conversation.

"Lots of construction in North Dakota. I saw that on Friday's update. I guess I'd stay south."

"Good plan. Thanks. Hope you find your man. I'll never get back to sleep now, so I think I'll take off."

"Sorry to have disturbed you, Doctor. Drive carefully. Lots of deer out at this hour."

"Not a problem. This is about my usual time anyway. Thank you, sir." Bryce stretched and exhaled with relief as the duo made their way back to their rig and exited the ramp.

After reattaching the wrist restraint and checking the Valium drip, Bryce slipped on vinyl gloves and changed Malandra's Attends. He dropped his garbage in the dumpster, washed up, refilled his travel mug from his thermos, and headed west. With the early start and plenty of caffeine, he calculated he could make it home in one long haul.

27

B Y MIDAFTERNOON, WELL INTO MONTANA, BRYCE COULD JUST make out a few snowcapped peaks of the Rockies on the distant horizon, and now he knew he could make it home by midnight. He picked up the burner phone and dialed. "Good afternoon, Mr. Carlyle. Detective Thompson here. I am ready to receive your documentation on the bone and hair samples. If you would be so kind as to FedEx them to me tomorrow, I can wrap this up."

"Of course, Detective. I already looked up the address of the Helena PD and have the packet ready to go."

"Uh, well, uh, you see, I thought I would have you send it directly to me so I can be certain of its arrival. I can't take the chance that it will get misplaced down at the station. I would rather sign for it myself."

"Chain of custody rules would be better served if it went directly from our lab to your department. As you know, when introduced in court, it must be shown that there was no interruption in the chain of custody, no chance someone could alter it or insert any confounding variables into the equation."

"Of course. Let me think." Bryce had involuntarily slowed the vehicle and drifted to the shoulder of the freeway, distracted by this curveball. "I am not supposed to report in for a couple of days, so please overnight it to my colleague, Detective Steven Willett. I already paid your secretary for same-day shipping. Willett can sign for it and maintain chain of custody."

"Perfect. It will be on tomorrow's plane."

"Thank you, Mr. Carlyle. You've been most helpful." Bryce ended the call and pulled back into the right lane. He thought for a minute, then pulled over and stopped the van on the shoulder of the road. He unlocked the gun safe and retrieved his personal cell phone, plugged it in, and powered it up.

"Willett here," a familiar voice answered on the second ring.

"Good afternoon, Detective. This is Bryce Thompson."

"Hello, Doctor. How are you doing?"

"Not too bad, considering. I have some information you need to know. I now have proof that Antonio Malandra killed his wife. Her parents found hair samples that we matched with samples in his possession, and there is a 99.9999 percent correlation. I realize you must think I have a vendetta against Malandra, but it was Bill, not me, who started this roller coaster.

"Now, although I can't prove any link between my family's deaths and Malandra's actions, he did have a laboratory setup in the basement of his home and somehow got it demolished one day before we went up there. I can swear to that in court. I saw it with my own eyes. My word against his, I realize, but when we put everything together, you will see there is only one conclusion possible."

"Can you come in and swear out an affidavit so we can pick him up for questioning?"

"No. There isn't time. I know where Malandra is hiding up in the mountains. He is making arrangements to leave the state. I will be making a citizen's arrest and charging him with the murder of his wife. You will be receiving a packet of information from a forensics lab in New York tomorrow. It was part of the investigation that Bill started," he said without lying. "That evidence will corroborate what I have just said. When you have it in hand, give me a call immediately, and I will do what I must do. He slipped away once. I'm not going to let that happen a second time."

"What if he has a gun? How are you going to handle him?"

"I have a plan for that. Trust me. I have thought this through for weeks now."

"OK. But I really don't like it. You could get hurt, or worse, if he is the kind of man you say he is."

"Oh, he is that kind of man. I do not believe I have ever met anyone so devious, so cunning, so ruthless as the good Doctor Malandra."

"I have no doubt you believe what you say. I just hope you can prove it and not get hurt. You've suffered enough already."

"Just call me at this number the minute you get that package from New York."

"Will do."

"Thank you, Detective. I'll wait for your call."

"Goodbye, Doctor Thompson. And be careful."

Shortly after 11 p.m., he was pulling into his driveway, and it suddenly hit him as hard as a blow across the jaw that he hadn't thought about how he would feel coming back to this empty house, a house full of ghosts and unfulfilled dreams. He sat there for several minutes, acclimating. A shudder ran through his body as he got out and opened the garage door, backed out Nicole's car, trying unsuccessfully not to inhale her scent, and pulled the van inside.

Pulling the IV from Malandra's hand and clipping the plastic ties, he changed the Attends one more time, dragged him to the back of the garage, secured his right arm to the workbench with Bill's handcuffs, and left him to sleep off the Valium remaining in his system. "You can sleep on cement tonight. You are not good enough to enter my wife's home."

Bryce took a deep breath and walked into the house, the quietude screaming at him from every corner. He was tempted to have a strong drink but told himself that would have to wait. He needed to stay sharp in case anything happened that he had to deal with, such as Malandra somehow getting to his feet and fighting or trashing the garage. That thought brought an idea with it. He found the set of bells that Nicole wore on her shoelaces when hiking in bear country. He hobbled Malandra's ankles with a nylon rope and tied the bells into the hobble. Any significant movement would alert him. Propping the door open to the garage, he wrestled his recliner to the archway of the living room and promptly fell into a much-needed slumber.

28

THE TINKLING OF BELLS TUESDAY MORNING ROUSED BRYCE JUST before seven, the latest he had slept in weeks. He walked to the open garage door and watched as Malandra struggled against his handcuffs. He looked awake but still dazed, gazing about, focusing, trying to figure out where he was and how he had gotten there. "Good morning, Tony. Welcome to Montana. We've missed you."

"What the hell are you doing, Thompson? You have no idea what you've done. You'll rot in jail for this. I'm going to sue you for every penny you have, and I will have the best goddamn team of lawyers money can buy."

"Oh, I'm sure you will. You can afford it. You can afford it just off the money you made on the Zebrowski hit, can't you?"

Malandra's face paled and went slack. Bryce could see in Malandra's expressionless glare that he knew his secret was no longer a secret.

"I can't prove you killed him, unless the grieving widow wants to turn on you to save her own skin."

"Bullshit."

"A rose by any other name …" Bryce trailed off as he went back into the kitchen and brewed a pot of coffee. He poured himself a cup, then poured a second one in a plastic mug and took it out to the garage along with a granola bar.

"Here you go. You must be hungry. You've only had sugar water for the past couple of days."

"Gee. Am I supposed to thank you now? You're too kind."

"I know I am. You're just lucky I don't believe in the death penalty, although the past few weeks have caused me to seriously question my logic." He took a sip of coffee and paced back and forth in the garage. "You, on the other hand, so consciously and constructively built your persona as the ethical man who did not believe in the death penalty while you toyed with the lives of others."

"I am innocent, and you can't prove shit. I'll walk. I guarantee it."

"OK. But I must warn you that you are under citizen's arrest. You have the right to remain silent. Anything you say can and will be held against you. You have the right to an attorney. If you can't afford an attorney, the court will provide one for you. There. Now you can't claim Miranda."

Bryce turned, scorn writ deep in his expression, and went back into the house. It felt good to shower and shave, but every little thing he touched or looked at held some memory of Nicole, especially in the master bedroom. He wasn't sure he could sleep in this room any longer. In fact, he wasn't sure he could live in this house any longer. He paced around, inside and out, for nearly three hours, unable to concentrate on anything but getting Malandra to justice. Finally, shortly after ten, his phone rang, and Willett's ID flashed on his screen.

"Hello, Detective. Did you get it?"

"I did. But I'm not sure what to do with it."

"I'll be there shortly, and everything will make sense once I explain the sequence of events to you. Meet me in the parking lot by the jailer's entrance."

"I'll be there."

Bryce walked to the garage and pulled a ball-peen hammer off the pegboard and slowly approached Malandra. "Do what I say, or I will hurt you. Got it?"

Malandra nodded.

"I am going to undo this handcuff and then cuff your hands behind your back. Then I will help you to your feet. The rope stays on your ankles. Understood?"

Malandra nodded again, his darting eyes betraying his intention to seek an out.

Bryce unlocked the handcuff from the workbench and pulled Malandra's arm behind his back. He started to resist but was weak and unsteady from the drugs and the inactivity of the last three days. Bryce quickly cuffed both wrists and raised Malandra to his feet. "Now, shuffle to the van and get inside. You'll have to sit on the step and swing your legs up. That hobble is too short for climbing." Malandra did as he was told, and Bryce quickly cuffed his ankle to the cot, opened the garage door, and headed the van downtown.

Detective Willett was standing in the parking lot with his assistant, Detective Shopp, as Bryce pulled alongside them. Bryce climbed in back and undid the leg cuff, then threw open the sliding door of the van. Jaws dropped when they looked inside. "Gentlemen, I am making a citizen's arrest and formally charging Antonio Malandra with the murder of Jill Downing-Malandra. He is responsible for the death of William Zebrowski and probably three to seven others in the past six years. However, there is nothing beyond conjecture on those cases, unless we can shake down Mrs. Zebrowski and offer her a plea deal that will get her talking. Either way, he will spend the rest of his life in prison, and society will be a safer place for it."

Malandra struggled against his restraints. "You aren't going to believe a lawbreaker, a kidnapper, over your own department's pathologist, are you? Think of all the times I have helped you guys. I want to make a formal complaint and citizen's arrest on this schizophrenic nutcase. He kidnapped me in New York and transported me across state lines. I have had every civil right you can think of violated."

"I'm sorry, Doctor Malandra, but the statutes are pretty clear on a citizen's arrest. We will have to take you inside pending investigation. We'll get the county attorney over here as soon as possible. If she thinks there is enough evidence, she will file for arrest and arraignment. Arraignment must happen within forty-eight hours by statute, barring unforeseeable circumstances like weather or natural disasters. You'll be out of here on bail tomorrow, two days at most."

"Then I can make a citizen's arrest on him for kidnapping me in New York?"

"A charge of kidnapping in New York is not in our jurisdiction. You will need to make that complaint in New York, and that will have to be addressed in a New York court."

"You have no evidence of anything. What can you possibly hold me on?"

"Doctor Malandra, I received a package today that includes, among other things, a notarized complaint from your deceased wife's parents along with some very troubling evidence from a forensics lab in Albany. Something Detective Bill Thompson was obviously working on before his untimely death."

"I want my phone call, and I want it now."

"Of course. Just come inside with us, and we'll get this figured out."

"I can't believe this. C'mon guys! You know me. You know I couldn't have done anything this guy is trying to accuse me of. We're on the same team. I'm one of you."

"I'm sorry, Doctor Malandra, but we must follow protocol. There's probably an explanation for all of this. It should be cleared up in a day or two. Let's go."

Bryce handed them his signed and notarized statement, a document he had worked on all week, and drove into the mountains, parking at the now-too-familiar trailhead. He walked up and down the meadow, talking aloud. "I got him, Nic. You hear that, Bill? I got him. Your instincts were right, again. I—no, we got him. He'll never hurt another person." He walked up and back, losing track of time, and finally left for the house.

Back home, he fixed an extra-large Crown Seven, went out to the back deck, and tried to enjoy the evening. Peering out over the back yard, all he seemed to see were the scores of ripening tomatoes bending the vines nearly to the ground with a bumper crop. And all he could hear were his words that fateful weekend when he told Nicole, "I promise. Later, we'll have more time. Then we can relax and enjoy life."

Later.

And then came the tears.

29

THE DOCKET WAS FULL, AND THE PRESIDING JUDGE HAD BEEN out on circuit, so Willett had told Bryce it could easily be two days before any arraignment was likely to take place. Thursday seemed an eternity away, but Bryce had waited this long. What was one extra day?

When his phone rang at four the next afternoon, he was surprised to see Willett's caller ID. "Hello?"

"Doctor Thompson, the county attorney would like to see you in her office. How far away are you?"

"I'm at the house. I can be there in a few minutes." He rang off and sped downtown to the county courthouse. *Must be some technical stuff they need information on. They won't set bail, so at least he will be in jail while they investigate all this. If they do consider bail, I'm ready to testify that Malandra has enough money to be a flight risk. I'm ready for them.*

What Bryce Thompson was not ready for was County Attorney Carolyn Goodwin. Obviously tired, her lids droopy, her hair in a bun that could be called less than tidy, and not a dab of makeup to lend her sallow face a hint of color, she was all business. She either did not notice Bryce's extended hand, or she ignored it on purpose, leaving him standing there, holding air.

"This is an extremely unusual case, and I have spent nearly the whole day working on it. Doctor Thompson, do you have an attorney?"

Bryce couldn't talk at first. His head was still in a bit of a daze, and he wasn't sure he had heard her correctly. "I beg your pardon?"

"I asked if you had legal counsel."

"No. Why would I need legal counsel?"

"Doctor Malandra has filed a brief for summary dismissal and is planning on filing an affidavit charging you with illegal entry, breaking and entering, assault, battery, impersonating an officer, kidnapping, illegal transportation across state lines, assault with a deadly weapon, and interstate conveyance while in commission of a felony, to name just a few, and I am advising you to have legal counsel at your side before you answer any questions."

Bryce was having trouble figuring out what was happening. His head was spinning.

"I don't understand. He killed his wife, and we have DNA evidence to prove that. I have had a conversation with the widow of a man he killed for the insurance money, and when my brother began investigating him, he killed my brother, my wife, and my unborn child. Why in God's name would I need legal counsel? He is the one going on trial here."

"The DNA evidence submitted against Antonio Malandra has no verification as to source, no location as to jurisdiction, no chain of custody, except your word against his. No one can verify where you obtained your sample. You are not a one-man wrecking crew. You could have gotten that tooth from anywhere. You did not go through proper legal channels. If we let every person in this country bring a vendetta against an adversary without proper legal precedent, I shudder to think what our legal system would come to, not to mention how bogged down we would be with frivolous claims."

"We, Detective Willett and I, can easily go to the hospital and verify the source of my evidence. There are still 206 bones and a mouth full of teeth that can be tested." Bryce began to relax now that he knew where to take this conversation. "On the way, I will call my attorney, and we can all meet back here in twenty to thirty minutes."

"That will work. I also understand from Detective Willett that you already claimed Doctor Malandra had a secret laboratory in his basement, only to find, with Doctor Malandra's full cooperation I might add, merely a workroom with an exhaust fan. I hope you have a little better evidence this time."

Bryce staggered over to Willett, his head spinning with the turn of events. "I don't know what just happened, but let's get over to the hospital."

"I knew something was up the minute she called me into her office. She is not too happy with the way this came down. She has worked with Malandra on multiple cases where his testimony was key. She has a very good track record, and she does not want a dirty case."

"I guess I'm an idiot when it comes to this legal crap. I thought evidence was evidence."

They walked to the parking lot as they talked. "You ride with me and call your attorney on the way. Have him meet us back here ASAP," Willett said. "And, no, evidence is not just evidence. There is good evidence, backed up by two or more officers and a documented chain of custody, that will hold up well in court. Then there is the bloody glove that could have been planted by a racist cop on the property of a black man, and a jury won't convict. It was Fuhrman's word against OJ's at that point. Unfortunately, that is what the county attorney is seeing here." They hopped in the car and, lights flashing, made good time to the hospital. Willett pulled up to the side entrance. "Let's go."

They walked to the pathology department, hot heels clicking on cold tiles, the staccato impatience echoing down the hall. When Bryce pushed the double doors open, his heart dropped as he froze mid-stride. There, where the graying bones of Eve had hung for years, was a brand-new, perfectly white, perfectly plastic, six-foot male skeleton. He burst into the office. "Where is the Eve skeleton?"

"Gone, Doctor Thompson," Melanie replied as she jolted against her backrest, startled by this brusque intrusion from the usually quiet physician. "That nice new one was just delivered a few days ago. The delivery company said the old one was getting brittle, and these new ones hold up much better. They said Eve was to be cremated. I guess Doctor Malandra took care of it."

"Where?"

"I have no idea."

"Do you have the name of the company?"

"No. He was in and out of here so fast, I didn't even catch his name. I never thought anything of it."

Bryce turned to Willett. "The skeleton that I got that sample from hung here for years. The DNA analysis was a perfect match to the hair samples from her parents in New York. You've got to believe me."

"Look, Doc, I know you are sincere and totally believe he killed her, but this is not going anywhere without corroborating evidence. We have to find something else to tie Malandra to a victim. Is there anything else?"

Bryce thought for a second, his mind racing. "The Zebrowski widow. I know where she lives. I was just there a few days ago and talked with her. She actually paid me to keep quiet when I told her I was part of the team that took out her husband. She got millions in life insurance, and Malandra took whatever percentage he agreed to. Let's go!"

Willett sped to the upscale housing development where Bryce had surprised Virginia Zebrowski two weeks earlier, but as they pulled onto the street, Bryce's heart fell again. In bold red and black, the sign in the front yard read "FOR SALE" and directed inquiries to the phone number of the realtor. They pulled into the driveway and checked the house, but it was locked and empty, the furniture gone, the rooms bare.

Bryce noticed a middle-aged man mowing his grass across the street and motioned for Willett to follow. As they approached the man, he idled his mower and wiped the sweat from his brow.

"Good morning. Can you tell me what happened to Mrs. Zebrowski across the street there?" Bryce asked, pointing to the empty house.

"Don't really know. Moving van just showed up a few days ago and moved her out in a few hours. The sign went up the same day. She hadn't been herself since her husband's death, and it didn't really surprise any of us here. Her best friend said she was talking about studying abroad, mentioned France, I guess, but left no forwarding address."

Bryce's head was a whirl of confusion. He didn't even thank the man and left Willett to extend that courtesy as he walked slowly back to the car. He slumped into his seat and waited for Willett to get in. "I should have guessed she might disappear once I busted her cover. And even if I did find her, it would be my word against hers."

"Sorry, Doc. I don't know what to say."

"He's going to get away with this, isn't he?"

Willett put the car in gear and started back toward East Broadway. "Without any further evidence, I don't know how we can hold him. That's the county attorney's call."

Back at the courthouse, Bryce paced in the hallway until his attorney arrived. He filled him in on the details, and then they entered the office and took a seat. Bryce held his breath as County Attorney Goodwin hustled in through her private entrance and took her place at the desk.

She straightened a stack of papers, set them purposefully off to the side, and began. "Doctor Thompson, we are here to discuss your complaint against Doctor Antonio Malandra and a most unconventional citizen's arrest, to say the least. Unless you can present further corroborating evidence, I find no grounds to hold Doctor Malandra any longer. He has no criminal record, owns a home and property worth two million dollars, and is not considered a flight risk. I therefore have no choice but to release him from custody."

She stared straight at Bryce. "Additionally, Doctor Malandra plans to press charges against you. He plans to file a complaint claiming he was in Hudson Falls, New York, not the mountains of Montana as you claim, when you assaulted him with force, committed battery, sedated him, then broke multiple federal laws when you kidnapped and transported him across multiple state lines. Nine, to be exact. Those allegations will have to await further investigation if and when he wishes to pursue it, but Doctor Malandra has been warned that the same standard for evidence holds per his charges against you. I understand your counsel has advised you to refrain from further statements until counsel has had time to prepare. If either of you wish to file a civil suit, that is a matter for a different venue and a different day. This meeting is over." She abruptly got up and left by her private entrance.

Bryce turned to his attorney. "Why don't you at least let me testify under oath? I could have possibly made a case to keep him in custody while we figured this out. I can't prove he killed my family, but we had proof that he murdered his wife. He's a goddam murderer, and he's going to walk."

"Jesus, Bryce. I'm a corporate lawyer. I do your taxes and your LLP stuff. I don't do defense and murder trials. We need to find you the right counsel. Lon Jepson will do this, I'm sure."

"Why do I need a defense lawyer? I haven't done anything but seek justice."

"Haven't you? Who allegedly broke into a house in New York and kidnapped Doctor Malandra, allegedly drugged him and drove him across God knows how many state lines, each one possibly a federal offense in its own right? It would have been malpractice for me to let you either incriminate yourself or perjure yourself. One slipup under oath, and you could serve time for a felony. I wouldn't ask you to do my heart bypass. Don't ask me to be your defense attorney in a possible felony assault and battery and kidnapping case."

"But I had the evidence. I could testify that the tooth came from the teaching skeleton everyone knew was in the path department for years, courtesy of Tony Malandra. It was a perfect match to the hair samples provided by the Downings from Jill's brush. We could have gotten the Downings out here, and they would have corroborated my story. There have been many innocent men sent to prison on less evidence than that. I don't get it."

"That's fine, and maybe that can still happen, but we need to do it by the book. You can't just take the law into your own hands. It makes you look like a lone-wolf vigilante, and the courts not only frown on such behavior, they take umbrage. They are not going to open that can of worms. If everyone was allowed to do that, it would be like the old west with every Tom, Dick, and Harry carrying a .45 and settling their disputes on Main Street. We need to put together a brief, and it needs to be loaded."

"You can have your loaded brief. I'll take my loaded .45. Christ, what a mess."

Detective Willett was leaving, and Bryce motioned to him as he passed. "Detective, thank you for trying. I just want to make sure you know that there is a high likelihood I will end up dead in the next few weeks. That's the kind of person we are dealing with here. I want you to promise me that if I die of some mysterious rare disease or accident, you will pursue that asshole to the ends of the earth."

"My God, you're serious, aren't you?"

"Have you forgotten my family? It's my fault for not involving you earlier, but none of you believed me. Like the day I took you up to see his lab. I swear there was a complete lab with a commercial, enclosed laboratory exhaust hood in that basement. I felt like you looked at me as just another grieving husband looking for a scapegoat."

"I'm sorry if I gave you that impression. Bill was a friend to all of us. We would have continued to investigate it. If everything you say is true, then you did a hell of a job getting that much put together in that short of time, but the system doesn't work that way. We would have had to put each piece in its place, then show the completed puzzle to the court."

"I know. I screwed up. I showed my hand too soon and gave him time to cover his tracks. I was afraid he would leave the country. I was thinking like a doctor, fighting a disease in real time with only minutes to save a life. I wasn't thinking like a cop. I thought the tooth and hair samples would seal the deal."

"Understood, but this isn't over. I, for one, do believe you. I'll take this as a personal challenge. For Bill. And Nicole. And the baby." He shook Bryce's hand and walked off.

Bryce thanked his attorney and then plodded to his car, feet heavy, head confused, heart empty.

30

WORK DIDN'T WORK. BRYCE WENT TO THE CLINIC AND DRAG-ged himself through the motions, but he knew he was no good. He couldn't concentrate. Worse, he couldn't care. When his last patient, Mrs. Vincent, waddled in for her diabetes follow-up on Thursday afternoon, he reviewed her numbers and let out a huge sigh. She had gained another six pounds, hadn't checked her blood sugar in two months, had promised to join the Y but "hadn't gotten around to it," and had forgotten to refill her meds for two weeks. Her fasting blood sugar was averaging 295, and all he could say was "You're slowly killing yourself, Betsy. Why don't you come back when you want to live?" He got up and walked out of the exam room, told his staff to clear his Friday schedule, and left for home.

The whiskey tasted too good splashed over ice and smoothed with 7UP, and he was on his third drink by six o'clock as he meandered through the garden, picking ripe tomatoes and eating them with a heavy shake of salt on each bite. The salt complimented the bittersweet drink, and the tomatoes complimented the bittersweet loneliness he felt each time he looked at Nicole's garden. He had promised to build it for her for two years but had been so busy that it was always "Later, there'll be time later." Now it was later, and he had nothing but time. He fixed another drink.

Hoping that the whiskey might ease the pain and help him forget, all it seemed to erase was everything but Nicole, everything that was extraneous, everything that wasn't worth remembering, leaving that glaring reality of just what it was he had lost. He sat on the reclining deck chair and finished another drink, then passed into a fitful sleep. His night was filled with dreams of climbing through a window, only to find that he was a hundred feet in the air with nothing to hang on to, no way down, and all he could see below were bones strewn across the ground, shreds of paper with strange words scrawled across them floating in the black air, and a tiny baby, no bigger than his hand, crawling into the bushes. The dream seemed to last until dawn, when he awoke, crept to the edge of the deck, and vomited until his stomach wrung itself dry with the last spasms. Bryce looked down into the grass and wondered if the red color was blood or merely tomato skins. In the dark light, he couldn't tell. In his dark head, he didn't care. He went into the house and collapsed on the bed.

Three hours of sleep, four ibuprofens, and a long hot shower later, he felt half human. He drove into the mountains to the wildflower meadow. Walking up and down the golden hillside, the mature grasses knee-high and swishing calmly against his legs, he tried to gain perspective as he talked out loud. "Tell me what to do, Hon. I don't have a clue what to do next. Where do I turn? I can't think straight. I can't concentrate. I can't work. I'm no good for anyone. You know me. All my life, I've felt the need to be relevant. And nothing seems relevant anymore. Nothing. I'm losing my mind, and I don't know what to do."

He sat on the boulder at the edge of the meadow for nearly two hours, but the swish, swish, swish of the tall grass was the only answer he received.

Returning to his pickup, he drove aimlessly for the next few hours. He couldn't recall where all he went, but near dusk, he found himself in Malandra's driveway, staring into the picture windows, the huge grizzly bear on the wall staring back at him, as if to say "I dare you."

Bryce didn't remember how he had gotten there or what he intended to do, but he sat and stared at the house for many long minutes, then turned around and left again. As he drove away, he saw a shadow in his rearview mirror walk to the window and stare out at him. "I'll be around, Tony boy. I'll be around, and I'll make sure you know it. You'll be looking over your shoulder, wondering where I'll show up next." He drove back to his house and opened another bottle of self-pity.

Bryce awoke the following morning with a pounding headache. It took him several seconds to realize someone was pounding on his front door. He splashed cold water in his face and brushed back his disheveled hair with wet hands, then shuffled to the door. Two men in dark suits were standing on his step, their eyes hidden behind dark sunglasses, no smiles or friendly gestures to greet him.

"Good morning. Are you Bryce Thompson?" the tall one asked.

"Yes. Who are you?"

"FBI," he answered as he flashed his badge.

Bryce's stomach was in his throat as he tried to respond. "What can I do for you?"

"May we ask you a few questions?"

"I … I guess so. What about?"

"Can you tell us where you were the third week of August?"

Bryce stammered and paused, shaken and unprepared for this, of all things. "I was camping up in the mountains, doing some scouting for an elk hunt this fall," he lied.

"Do you own a white Ford van?"

"I did. But I sold it."

"May I ask why you bought and sold it so quickly?"

Sweat was beading on Bryce's forehead and upper lip as he tried to collect his wits. "I had planned to do some cross-country vacationing, saving money by sleeping in the van. But it wasn't working out. I decided I needed something bigger, that's all."

"I see," the agent said unconvincingly as he jotted notes in a pocket-sized notebook. "And where all did you go with this van?"

"Up in the mountains for a trial run. Look. What's this all about? I am a law-abiding citizen with no criminal record, minding my own business. I believe I have the right to have a lawyer present, don't I?"

"You may, if you think you need one," the agent said, drawing out the words very slowly, no real expression in his glare, although Bryce thought he caught hint of a smirk. "We are just following up on a complaint. I have reason to believe you know about it, and I think you know who filed it. Kidnapping is a federal offense," he added, gauging Bryce's reaction. "That's why we were called in."

"I have been advised by legal counsel not to say anything without them present, so if you would like to set up a meeting, I would be happy to cooperate. His name is Lon Jepson. We could meet at his office when he has an opening in his schedule."

The agent jotted something in his notebook. "We still have a bit of fact finding to do. Don't try to leave town. When we are ready, we will give Jepson a call, and both of you can meet us at precinct headquarters," the second agent added, making sure Bryce knew who was in charge and who would set the agenda. "We'll be around," he added as they turned and walked to their car.

31

THE NEXT DAYS WERE WORSE THAN EVER. BRYCE WAS CONSTANTLY looking over one shoulder, waiting for Malandra to silence him, and the other shoulder, waiting for the FBI to arrest him. He felt compressed, unable to move, unable to breathe freely. Worse, he felt stupid, thinking he had been so smart to bring Malandra to justice, as if a citizen's arrest was so easy. He had fouled the investigation, and the skeletal remains had disappeared. Now, it was his word against Malandra's on exactly where that tooth DNA came from, even though he had Tim and Monica Downing's evidence and affidavit to back him up. However, the county attorney and the chief wanted none of it. Tony was their friend, and they controlled the agenda. And to top it off, Bryce was now the subject of a federal investigation. How could it get any worse? He returned home after another fruitless day and opened a bottle of wine, sat on the deck, and tried to forget.

Unfortunately, it didn't work. Worse than the FBI lurking in his shadows, the dreams kept coming, no matter how much wine or expensive whiskey he used to numb his neurons. The dreams were different each night, though eerily the same. Often a different setting, always a different chronology, still, each had him perched on a windowsill or a narrow ledge, stranded high in the air. Below, he could see the scattered bones, the pieces of paper floating through the air carrying the illegible words, and the baby crawling away, always away, always faceless, fading into the distance. What was worse, the dreams started to fill his head in the daylight, strange things haunting his thoughts even while he tried to work. He worked through his patients at the clinic the next week, but he could not have told anyone whom he had seen or what he had prescribed. He was going through the paces, but he was not engaged.

A week into this living nightmare, his attorney called. "Bryce, I just received a call from an FBI agent. He wants to meet with us at police headquarters at four this afternoon. Can you make it to my office by three so we can discuss our response?"

"Of course. I'll move some patients and be there. I don't have a choice. I need to get this over with and behind me." He cleared his schedule and was at Jepson's office by three.

"What should I do?" He asked Jepson, pacing the room, too animated to sit down. "I told them I was camping and sleeping in my van. That is not a lie. I said I was scouting for an elk hunt this fall. I hunt every fall, and I actually was in the mountains that week, so that's not a lie. I did bring Malandra down the highway from those very mountains when I made the citizen's arrest. That's not a lie. Do I plead the fifth beyond that?"

They talked things over for nearly an hour. Finally, Jepson said, "No matter what you tell them, make sure each statement can stand alone and is true. The more you jabber on, the more likely it is that they can catch you in a contradiction. And lying to federal agents is a crime in itself. That's about all we can do. It's nearly four. Let's go."

To Bryce's immense relief, when they arrived at headquarters, Willett was there as well, sitting in the interview room with the agents, laughing and making small talk.

They took their seats. The tall agent was the first to speak. "Our investigation has turned up nothing suspicious, Doctor Thompson. We got a warrant for your phone records, and your cell phone never pinged all that week. When it did ping, it was off a tower high in the mountains to the east. We accept your answer that you were camping and out of range. Your phone never pinged once out of state, so we have no evidence that you were in New York as Malandra claims.

"Additionally, we searched your credit card history, and there were no out-of-state purchases that week. In fact, there were no purchases at all that week except for one gas and one grocery receipt here in town right before you went camping. That all fits with your chronology.

"But just as importantly, Detective Willett has been very helpful, and he has corroborated your story and your whereabouts up in the mountains that week. He has assured us that everything you did, you did because you are convinced that Malandra killed his wife, as well as your pregnant wife and your brother. The same brother who was his senior detective and good friend. If we have a cop killer out there, we want to help this department as much as we can.

"It appears that you were where you said you were, and we have no evidence to the contrary. We have no further questions for you at this time, Doctor Thompson, but we may have to follow up in the future. In the meantime, you stay in touch with Willett, and do not do anything unless he approves. Are we okay with this?"

Relief washed over Bryce like a cool shower on a summer day. He tried not to look at Willett, tried not to show the questioning in his face. "That works for me," he said, turning to Jepson.

Jepson echoed his agreement, relieved that somehow Willett had forestalled a potential disaster with his client. "Call me if anything new comes up," Jepson added as he left for his office.

Willett thanked the agents and then walked Bryce to his vehicle. "We need to talk, Doc," he said when they were alone in the parking lot. "I covered for you as best I could. I told the truth as I knew it, but if this goes any further, I won't lie under oath. Every statement I made to them was true. I just left out a few details," he added with his sly grin. "I need you to keep this absolutely between me and you. Absolutely no one else can know we talked, or my job could be on the line. If we can somehow get more evidence on Malandra, this will go away."

"I don't know how to thank you. My God, I thought I was in deep trouble. Federal charges, no less."

"I owed Bill a lot of favors. It was the least I could do. But it's not over until it's over, so keep your nose clean and don't talk to anyone. We can't trust anyone to keep a secret. Got it?"

"Got it." Bryce shook his hand in an extended grasp, his heavy burden lightened a bit, and headed for home.

The next few days went better, and as time passed, he began to get into his old routine, although he turned his hospital patients over to one of his partners. He avoided the hospital, afraid that he might lose it if he ran into Malandra in the hallways. One morning, as the nurses were peppering him with questions and preparing for the day, Bev handed him a cup of coffee and asked if he had heard the news.

"What news?"

"Doctor Malandra turned in his resignation."

"Is he still in town?"

"No one knows. Nobody's seen him for days."

Bryce grabbed his phone and hit Detective Willett's number.

"Willett here."

"Tony Malandra has resigned at the hospital. Have you heard anything? Has he blown town?"

"No, I hadn't heard a thing."

"What now? The legal system won't do anything without more proof. How do we get him now?"

"Honestly, Doc, I don't know what to tell you."

"You're the only one who believes me. Can you at least drive up to his place and see if he's even around?"

"Sure. I'll do that right now. I'll call you within the hour."

"Thanks." Bryce rung off and slumped in his chair. *Gone. Slipped the hangman.*

He plodded through the next several patient visits, trying to concentrate, and finally Willett called back.

"Sorry it took so long, Doc, but there's no good news. The place is locked up, and there's a for sale sign in the yard. I contacted the realtor, and she said it was one of the strangest deals she has ever had. She said he didn't really care about the sale price, just said to move it fast and wire the money to his bank."

"What bank? Where?"

"She wasn't really at liberty to say, but she hinted that it might be Swiss."

"That fits. Bill was suspicious that Malandra was too rich for his age. He told me that Malandra had flown to Switzerland on more than one occasion. I shouldn't have doubted him."

"I don't know what to say, but I don't think there is anything more I can do."

"Can you do me one more favor? Can you call the police chief in Hudson Falls, New York, and ask him to call on Francis Malandra? She lives at 110 Elm Street. Just have him find out if Tony went back there. That's all I ask. At least that way we'll know where to find him if we come up with more evidence."

"Sure. I can do that. No problem."

"By the way, any info on the Zebrowski widow? Where she took off to? She might be our last hope, and even then, she admitted she never saw him. Only phone calls."

"Nothing. She's disappeared. Vanished. We're querying the airlines, but that takes a while, even assuming she traveled under her own name and on a domestic carrier. If she went into Canada and took a foreign carrier like Emirates or Qatar, especially under a different name, we'll never trace her."

"Any word on that skeleton? Any info on the company that picked it up and dropped off the new plastic one?"

"Detective Shopp has been working on that. It's a company out of Salt Lake. He talked to one of the managers, and he said it's already been cremated and the ashes picked up. He tried to get permission from the chief to drive down there and see if he could find anything more concrete, but the chief said we're done wasting time on this. The guy he talked to said he couldn't read the signature on the receipt. It was marked "Paid. Cash." The receipt was made out to a John Smith. Real original, huh?"

"Of course it's already been destroyed. He's got every track covered, hasn't he?"

"Sorry, Doc. I don't know what else we can do. I'm out of ideas."

"Just call New York, OK? I don't know what to do either, but I want to know where the son of a bitch is hiding out in case something new turns up."

"Will do."

Bryce slogged through his clinic, then headed straight home. He bypassed the kitchen and went straight to his office. He had been taking double doses of antacids and had lost ten pounds since the funerals, but food still did not appeal to him. Cooking for one or just being in the kitchen reminded him too much of Nicole. He sat at his desk and powered up the little camera cabled to his iMac. He fast-forwarded to the video of Francis Malandra's back room and hit the freeze-frame button when he got to the pictures of the desk. He panned slowly, looking at the papers on the desk that he had so cautiously avoided moving, now wishing he had taken more time, gotten more information, but just as he was chastising himself, there, behind a receipt for groceries, he could see the top half of a letter-head. Jacksonville Realty. He zoomed in.

"Dear Dr. Malandra.

"We believe you will find this property in the beach area south of city center to your liking. Away from traffic noise, Seascape Unit 805 is a corner unit with a beautiful view of the ocean, the most spec-tacular sunrises reflected across endless expanses of ocean waves. A one-year lease-to-own contract is available, and we are confident that this is ..."

The grocery receipt covered up the lower part of the letter, but at least it was something. It may have just narrowed the search from the entire United States to a few square miles in Florida. Next, Bryce brought up the website of the Duval County Clerk of Courts, lim-ited his query to the past two years, and after a short search, found two entries for Antonio Malandra. One referenced a decedent and property claim of the widow, the second a title insurance search for a condominium south of Jacksonville. *Time to consult Google Earth.*

In no time, he had Seascape Condominiums brought up on his screen. The beautiful curving lines of the construction, the large balconies, the ample parking lot and parking garage, and the pure white, pristine beach just beyond the sidewalks were all laid out for him to see. Bryce printed the address and stored the pictures in his long-term memory.

An idea had prodded his thoughts weeks earlier, and now he put it into action. The pen digital recorder, shaped and sized like any other ballpoint pen, had arrived from SpyGuy but had gone unused. He made sure it was charged, then called Willett again.

"Sorry to bother you, Detective, but can I meet you somewhere? I promise I'll be brief."

"Sure. I was just heading home, but I could meet you in the hospital parking lot. It's right on the way."

"Perfect. I'll be there in five minutes."

Minutes later, Bryce was speeding into the parking lot where Willett was standing by his car. He hopped out and shook Willett's hand. "Thank you again. Sorry to bother you, but I knew I couldn't sleep all weekend without direction from you. Any news from New York?"

"There is no one at Mrs. Malandra's house except a very lonely widow. She started crying when the sheriff questioned her about her son's whereabouts. She was alone, he was very certain of that. So, what's up?"

"Suppose I could find Tony Malandra and get him alone, one on one, and get him to talk, get him to incriminate himself, and get it recorded? If we coupled that with my sworn testimony that the tooth came from his skeleton and matched perfectly with the hair samples from New York, would that be enough to convict him of his wife's murder?"

"I don't know. You never know what a jury will do or what a judge will allow, but it's possible. What exactly do you have up your sleeve?"

"I may have found out where he is. I won't try to make another citizen's arrest. I promise. But if I can get him to talk, it will be up to you to have him extradited."

"How are you going to get it recorded?"

Bryce pulled the pen out of his pocket and connected its headphones, then handed one of the earpieces to Willett and hit playback.

"I don't know. You never know what a jury will do or what a judge will allow, but it's possible. What exactly do you have up your sleeve?" Willett's face lit up when he heard his own voice as clear as if he was standing there talking.

"That's remarkable. Where did you get that little toy?"

"A quick internet search and two hundred dollars. When I'm done with it, it's yours as a gift for all the trouble I've caused you."

"You don't need to do that, but it's pretty cool. I would never have given it a second look."

"I won't have any use for it after this, but you might. I just hope I can find him."

"Where did you get the lead?"

"Suffice it to say it was something Bill had uncovered that gave me the lead."

"Okay."

"Just promise me that you will pursue this if I get more damning information. He'll fight extradition, and you will need to be persistent."

"You get me a confession on tape, and, believe me, the whole force will be behind bringing a cop killer to justice. Bill was more than respected on the force. He was a friend to all of us. We can only imagine the loss you feel, losing your entire family. Unimaginable!"

"Bill was convinced that Malandra had a dark side, and when he pushed, it cost him his life. I only wish I had listened to him. I lay in bed at night trying to think what I could have done differently, but I just never saw it coming."

"I have to admit I thought you were going a bit loco when you took me to his basement to show me his secret lab, only to find a paint shop. But you will swear under oath that those pictures were taken at his house just two days before, right?"

"Without hesitation. If we could have gotten the search warrant the day before, we might have had him. It's all so clear in hindsight. Who would have thought he could have transformed it so fast? And had his security tapes wiped clean, as well."

"Yeah. I've been thinking about that. He must have had a second set already set up. He had them ready way too fast. He must have been planning for that type of cover-up. How he edited the dating is beyond me. He's smart. I'll give him that much."

"Oh, yeah. Summa cum laude smart. But that doesn't mean he's innocent," Bryce added.

"Christ, no. Some of the worst criminals have some of the most brilliant minds. But they don't think like average people. They begin to think that rules apply to the herd, but not to them. They are problem solvers, and one of the problems they have to solve is how to outwit the other 99.99 percent of society. It becomes a game to them, and their satisfaction is not in socially acceptable accomplishments but in winning their game. Not to mention the power it gives them over others."

"Precisely. Serial killers often admit that taking a life gives them a thrill they can't match any other way. They will declare that they don't want to keep doing it, that they want to be normal, but the compulsion drives them back again and again."

"That's something I've never been able to get my head around, even after all my years on the force. How can torturing a person or taking someone's life give them the thrill, the high, the ecstasy they feel?"

"Their brains are wired differently. Wolf versus rabbit. That much I'm sure of. Now, I need to get going. Thank you for your help. Wish me luck."

"Be careful," Willett said as he offered his hand. "Please be careful."

"I will. I don't plan a confrontation this time. I just want to get him talking. Megalomaniacs love to tell of their exploits. He loves to talk about his hunting trophies; the more dangerous, the better. He probably wants to tell me." Bryce shook Willett's hand and headed to his car. Over his shoulder, he added, "He probably needs to tell me."

32

"Thompson, William. Business Class. Jacksonville." He said it quietly, like he did it every day, even though the butterflies were active as he handed the flight agent Bill's ID. "Police. Not carrying." Bill's driver's license picture was clean-shaven. Bryce's three day's growth and hat pulled low on his forehead caused no hesitation for the agent, the family resemblance firm. She handed him his boarding pass, and he filed down the line, a mental picture of sheep coming to mind.

He had considered flying his own plane to Florida—less hassle and nearly as quick—with no time wasted in security and check-in lines, but that would leave a paper trail too easy to follow. He wanted to be invisible, just like in New York. Plenty of cash would allow him to use Uber and taxis, no rental car hassles or paperwork, and a new no-contract phone would help him remain incognito, just like in New York. His transfers went seamlessly, bypassing luggage lines with his lone carry-on, and he was grabbing a ride in Jacksonville by early afternoon. He gave the driver the address of a run-down hotel near the condos where he believed Malandra was living and asked him to wait.

"I'll only be a few minutes," he said as he paid his fare and hustled inside. After checking in and stashing his things in the room, he hopped back in the car and gave him the address of the Seascape Condominiums. Memorizing the streets and buildings as they drove, he was there in less than two minutes, an easy walk to and from his hotel. Bryce strolled the entire perimeter of the huge property, sunglasses in place and Panama pulled low over his eyebrows. He had never been to Florida in the summer, and he was already second-guessing his strategy. The heat index was hovering around one hundred, and Bryce was wishing he had brought cooler clothes. He walked along the beachfront, a gentle breeze whispering off the water, but needed to return to the opposite side where he could monitor the parking lots, his best chance of spotting Malandra. Finding some shade where he could view the parking lots using his camera with the 500-mm telephoto lens, he was already rethinking his decision not to get a rental car with air-conditioning. The heat was bad enough this early evening. What would it be like at midafternoon?

Bryce paced the shady side of the street across from the condos but realized he was too exposed. A few minutes here and there was one thing, but a lone man standing in the street for hours on end was not going to work. He ambled down to a small restaurant on the corner where he had a view of the condo building. He found a window booth and ordered an iced tea. This would work for a while, but he couldn't sit here all day. He would probably have to rent a car after all. Panning his camera across the eighth floor yielded no activity, most of the drapes closed against the summer heat. He watched for people coming and going from the main entrance doors and the parking lots, but no familiar face was to be seen. He ordered a soda and a burger, waiting as long as he could in the cool interior. Toward dusk, he again walked the east side of the complex along the edge of the water, occasionally slipping into the shade of a palm tree and scanning the eighth-floor windows, the westering sun finally yielding its intensity. Devoid of any activity useful to him, he ambled around the property until dark, when lights began coming on in the building, but well past dark, drapes were still drawn, and Bryce was still empty-handed.

As he took a long, cool shower, he tried to think of a better plan. He couldn't stay out all day in this heat and humidity. He would have to rent a car.

It had cooled precious little overnight, and as the rose-colored sky brightened toward the yellow spectrum over the graying Atlantic, the mercury oozed relentlessly skyward. Up early per his usual, Bryce took a cab to a rental car lot and signed for a small compact. The bored guy behind the desk barely looked at the driver's license and passport as he filled out the papers for Thompson, William. Bryce paid cash and included refueling and insurance coverage, just in case.

Bryce grabbed breakfast at the corner restaurant, killing an hour, then sat in his air-conditioned rental and searched the eighth-floor windows for activity. The curtains were all pulled against the Florida sun, and he learned nothing. He walked to the entrance of the condo unit and loitered near the secured entrance, pretending to read the newspaper he held. When a couple walked out, Bryce quickly slipped inside before the door closed.

He strolled around the ground floor, examining the layout and studying the mailboxes. There was no name on #805. He considered taking the elevator to the eighth floor but noticed a woman entering the elevator and using her card key to actuate the buttons. *Too much security.* He headed back to his car and waited. Day number two passed with no luck, and he was well into day number three, sitting in the air-conditioned rental, when the back door of his car opened. It dawned on him too late that the doors automatically unlocked when he put the car in park. The car rocked as someone hopped inside. As he turned to look, Bryce felt hard metal against the back of his neck.

"You truly are not a quick learner, are you, Thompson? Don't turn around, and don't make any quick moves."

The unmistakable voice of Tony Malandra would have frozen Bryce even without the cold barrel of a pistol against his skin. "Good morning, Doctor Malandra." He said it with emphasis after he slowly reached for his left breast pocket and turned on the recording pen. "To what do I owe the honor of this visit?"

"Maybe I should be saying the same thing," Malandra answered, his voice barely a whisper. "Was I just supposed to sit on my haunches and wait to be kidnapped again?"

"That's being a tad paranoid for an innocent man, isn't it, Tony?"

"Of course I'm paranoid, with a schizo like you hounding me. I figured you would show up. You're as persistent as you are stupid. It didn't cost me that much to have you watched and be alerted with a text when you dropped out of sight in Montana."

"And just how did you pull that off. Paid informant on the force?"

"Much simpler than that. And much cheaper. I got a text every night at ten confirming that you were in Montana. Drug addicts will do almost anything for a quick few hundred. Then three days in a row, the texts inform that you haven't been seen. I look out my window with my spotting scope and see a tourist with a huge camera spending far too much time on the wrong side of the building. I focus my forty-power lens and see a face from the past, unmistakable despite the hat and sunglasses. And I say, 'He's dumber than I thought.'"

"Yes, Tony. You are the only smart one. You are smarter than everyone, as you keep reminding us. That is why you feel you have the right to kill the inferior. 'Culling the herd strengthens the species,' as you put it. But I didn't know until a few weeks ago that you meant the human herd as well. Incidentally, what caliber is that you have aimed at me?" he asked, certain he was talking loud enough for the recorder.

"It's only a .38 with a silencer but plenty enough at this range. It won't kill you instantly like a .44 might, but with a severed spine and internal hemorrhaging, you wouldn't last long."

"The only thing I ask is, why did you do it? My brother. My wife. Did you know she was pregnant, Tony? Why?" Bryce said as he adjusted the rearview mirror, trying to see if there was any emotion in Malandra's face. That face revealed none.

"How was I to know he was your brother?"

"But why Bill? Couldn't you outsmart him?"

"He was threatening my very existence, and when that happens in the jungle, the strong survive, and the weak die. It's just the way it is. Every second of every day, something must die so something else can eat. That is the only law of survival." He pressed the gun harder into Bryce's neck. "Now, let's go for a drive, so we can talk this over. This is no place for a negotiation."

"I would love to, but I'm much more comfortable out here in the open. If I end up in the country, I'll never see the light of day again."

"I could just end this conversation right now and be gone in a second. It happens all the time in Florida. No one here gives a shit about one stranger, more or less. Now, pull out of this parking lot and head south. I'm sure we can make some sort of deal, work something out."

Bryce winced as Malandra slammed the gun deeper into his flesh. He put the car into gear and backed out of his parking space, cruising slowly toward the street exit, eyeing his surroundings. Spotting a car coming from the north and a foursome of vacationers crossing the street at the intersection, Bryce stepped on the gas and roared into the street. He stopped just short of the oncoming car, slamming the gear into park as he simultaneously opened his door and fell to the pavement. He jerked rhythmically and forced spittle into a froth spewing from his pursed lips.

"Oh, my God!" the woman at the front of the tourist group screamed as traffic slid to a stop just feet away from where they were walking. "He's having a seizure. Phil. Call 911!"

"No!" Malandra hollered as he jumped out of the back seat. "That won't be necessary. He'll come out of it on his own." But the woman's husband, duly instructed, was already dialing.

"Protect his head," she yelled as Malandra fumbled to secret his gun back under his shirt. When she realized Malandra was not going to act, she scrambled to Bryce's side and cradled his head in both hands, keeping the jerking head off the cement. As the seizure activity began to subside, she turned to her group. "Let's get him off the middle of the road before we have a total traffic jam," she said as oncoming traffic slowed near the commotion. The four people gently slid Bryce to the sidewalk as Malandra stole away.

Minutes later, red lights and sirens cleared the street as a police cruiser and an ambulance screeched to a stop next to the now quiet body. Bryce peeked through nearly closed lids, making certain Malandra was nowhere in sight, then let the crew load him onto the gurney and into the back of the ambulance before he spoke. "I'll be okay, guys. Just got a bit overheated."

"That's fine, sir. Just relax, and we'll check you out." The medic began studying Bryce's arms for an IV site as his partner checked blood pressure and pulse.

"I don't need an IV, guys. I'll be fine."

"Just let us do our job, sir."

"Actually, I have the right to refuse an IV. And I am refusing an IV right now."

By now, the gurney had been locked in place, and the driver was ready to pull away from the curb. "My place is right around this corner. I insist on getting out. It is my right to refuse treatment."

The medic looked at the team leader and shrugged. The team leader finished listening to Bryce's heart and lungs, checked his pupils and hand-eye coordination, then motioned for the driver to wait. "You will have to sign this form saying you refused medical treatment. That you left against medical advice. If something bad happens, you acknowledge that you accept full responsibility and you release us from liability."

"Believe me, I understand better than you know." He scrawled an illegible line on the form, looked through the ambulance windows to make sure Malandra wasn't around, and then hopped out. He told the police officer directing traffic that he was just overheated, then jumped into the rental car and drove to the hotel. He threw his things into his duffel and headed to the airport. By midnight, he was back in Montana.

33

EIGHT IN THE MORNING FOUND BRYCE IN THE PARKING LOT OF the police station awaiting Willett's arrival. The unmarked tan car was by now too familiar to Bryce, and he stepped out of his vehicle as soon as he saw it pull in.

"Back so soon?" Willett asked. "Any luck?"

"Some, I think. He was waiting for me. Had some druggie informant calling him with my whereabouts. Caught me off guard, but I got him to talk a little. You be the judge," he added as they grabbed a cup of coffee and retreated to Willet's office.

Willett listened to what Bryce had recorded. "Out of context, it doesn't mean he's guilty, but within the context of what we know, it takes on a different flavor. I'll take this to the county attorney. It's up to her to determine if we have enough to even bring charges, let alone pursue an extradition order. Don't get your hopes up too much. The chief and the county attorney were friends with Malandra."

"She was none too happy with me, I have to admit."

"You kind of ran over his civil rights."

"And he never ran over my family's civil rights?"

"Of course he did, if he's guilty. But that's the big if, according to the law, and you have no concrete proof. When that happens, even the guilty walk."

"What you're telling me is that, barring further concrete evidence, the legal system won't help me. And I can't take the law into my own hands, or the legal system will prosecute me."

"I'll call you as soon as they listen to this, but I'm afraid you're right."

Bryce handed him the pen and the ear buds. "Keep it. Maybe you can get some use out of it."

"Thanks." Willett took Bryce's hand in an extended handshake and walked him to the door. "Our system usually works. It has evolved to protect the innocent. Remember how awful justice was in the Middle Ages? A noble could accuse a peasant of theft and have him flogged or hung at his whim with absolutely no proof and no repercussions. The framers of our Constitution were learned men who understood that history and did not want it repeated. Without evidence beyond a reasonable doubt, an occasional guilty party is bound to go free so ten innocent ones don't suffer in jail. That's the way it is. That's the way it must be, if we are to remain a free people."

Bryce left the building, and a part of him knew it was for the last time. He had nothing left for the law, and they had nothing left for him. He went to the clinic and went through mail, trying to clean up his desk. If only, he thought, he could as easily clean up his life. He sat at his desk and stared out the window looking over the valley. He had a great practice; he had money; he had a beautiful home; he was good-looking and popular. He had it all. Almost. Without his family, he had nothing.

Detective Willet dropped by the clinic two hours later. "Sorry, Doctor Thompson, but it's just as I suspected. Goodwin says this is still totally circumstantial, your word against his. Without something more direct, her decision stands."

"Sure. Thanks for trying. Amazing, when you think about it, how much power a prosecutor has. I don't get the opportunity to get up on the stand under oath and make my case against a cold-blooded murderer, and it all hinges on one person's opinion."

"It's not perfect, but it's our system. I just want you to know that I believe you. Unfortunately, I may be the only one who believes you. Chief Murphy thinks you're a bit weirded out over the loss of your family. 'Overreacting' was his word. Taking the law into your own hands. On top of that, they're all friends, so they naturally trust Malandra over you."

"So, everyone is treated equally, but some are treated more equally. Right?"

"Afraid so. That's the human element. They're not going to prosecute a friend without hard, cold evidence. That bar is much higher than for some loser off the street with a criminal record."

"So, that's it?"

"Well, not necessarily," Willett said with a sly twinkle in his eyes. "I haven't mentioned this to the chief, but I've made a call to Jacksonville, started a rapport with one of the detectives there, asked him to watch Malandra a bit. And he was more than willing to help when I mentioned the words 'cop killer' to him. This whole thing has my head in a spin. Keep this to yourself, okay?" Willett added, his voice suddenly lowered. "My brother is an engineer in Daytona Beach. I have some PTO coming, and I keep promising him I'll come down for a visit. It's not far from there to Jacksonville. I might just have to drive up and have a look for myself, anonymously of course. Watch him a little. Maybe listen in on some phone calls?" he added, unable to hide the grin that wrinkled the normally unflappable demeanor.

"I appreciate the effort more than you know. And thanks for believing me, but I have a feeling there is nothing more we can do. I'm afraid he's won."

"Maybe. We'll see. I'll let you know if and when I know something."

"Thanks, and good luck, Detective."

As he closed the door, he had the sense that he had closed the door on the whole affair. He knew Willett believed him, and that was comforting, but he also feared that Willett could not help him. They were done. He told the front desk to book appointments starting on Monday and left for home.

34

No matter how much he medicated himself, Bryce could not stop the dreams. They haunted him night after night, and every morning he woke with a headache and a promise to stay sober, which he did for ten to twelve hours, but as darkness fell, outside and within, he would fix one small drink and sit on the back deck trying to figure out what to do with the rest of his life. When the answers failed to materialize, he would fix just one more small drink, Crown Royal with 7UP or Woodford over ice. Oh, how good that first one tasted, even better with the second. And after the second, he had lost the fight for one more night.

Bryce did fine when he was at work, concentrating on disease and medications, diagnoses and treatments, but it was when he was alone, so alone, that the hauntings began. Some nights, he would sleep at the hospital so as not to be so isolated, and there was no temptation to self-medicate when he was on the job. Work was his salve, and over the next two weeks, he was putting in around a hundred hours per week and taking extra call for his partners, much to their delight. But at night, alone, trying to sleep, that was when the demons came out.

The dreams, different each time yet eerily the same, taunted him. He would awaken, unrefreshed, wondering when they would end.

It was on the third week of this marathon that Detective Shopp met him in the parking lot of the hospital when he arrived for morning rounds. "Good morning, Doctor Thompson. Have you heard the news?"

"What news?"

"About Detective Willett?"

"No. He hasn't been in touch. Did he find something in Florida?"

"No. He was found dead in a hotel room in Jacksonville."

"You've got to be shitting me!" Bryce slumped against his car, his legs rubber.

"It was totally bad luck if ever there was bad luck," Shopp added. "No foul play. I'm sure that's what you are thinking. They did an autopsy and found a tick in his armpit. Toxicologies are still pending, but the preliminary report lists it as probable tick disease. They called it some kind of tick toxin."

"Tick paralysis."

"I talked to his brother. He said he was fine the evening before. He talked to him on the phone around 9 p.m., and nothing seemed out of the ordinary. Housekeeping found him the next morning. Died in his sleep."

"Tick paralysis doesn't kill that fast. They usually get muscle weakness in the limbs and gradually worsen for twenty-four to forty-eight hours. Then, as the toxin is further released from prolonged tick feeding, they get more central weakness until the respiratory muscles fail. It takes days."

"I don't know anything about the medical stuff, but I scanned the autopsy report my contact in Florida sent me. They found an engorged tick in his armpit and confirmed death due to muscle weakness and respiratory arrest. There was no struggle, no bruising, no sign of foul play."

"Did he tell you why he went to Florida?"

"Yeah. His brother lives there, and he had vacation time coming."

"His brother lives in Daytona Beach. Did he tell you why he was going up to Jacksonville?"

"No."

"Doctor Tony Malandra is living in a condo in Jacksonville. He went up there to see what he was up to, do a little undercover stuff, see if he could get any information that would help our case here."

"Wow."

"Did they identify the tick? Genus and species? Was it mentioned in the report?"

"I don't remember seeing it. Why?"

"The only tick that kills that fast is the Australian paralysis tick. The North American form of the disease is carried mostly by the dog tick and the Rocky Mountain tick, and the disease comes on gradually. Most often, the tick is found and removed, and the toxin wears off. It isn't usually fatal, although it can be in rare cases. I read up on it when Bill asked me to help him on a project. There have only been about fifty fatal cases reported in the last fifty years in the U.S. It's rare, but we just happened to have had one right here in Helena a couple of years ago. What a coincidence." He looked Shopp directly in the eyes for a long minute. "You guys are crazy if you think Willett died from tick paralysis in a matter of hours. Tony Malandra killed him. Just like he kills anyone who gets in his way."

"What do you want me to do?"

"Get me a copy of that autopsy report. And call the hotel where he was staying. Find out how housekeeping found him. Find out if his room was dead bolted or safety chained. Did they have to force their way in? Wouldn't a cop use his safety locks? Wouldn't you? I'll bet you a C-note that door was not locked from the inside."

"I see where you're going with this. I'll get on it right now. Thanks, Doc."

"I want to talk to the chief about this. You get what information you can, and I'll meet you at headquarters over noon hour, if that's okay with you."

"Perfect. Thank you!"

Bryce made rounds and saw his morning patients, then hurried to the station where Detective Shopp was waiting for him. "The chief is expecting us," he said as he led him to the back office.

"Good afternoon, Doctor Thompson. Shopp has filled me in a bit. What's on your mind?"

"Did you print a copy of the autopsy prelim?"

"Yes, it's right here," he said as he handed Bryce a small stack of papers.

Bryce flipped through the report until he found the section he was looking for. "Here it is. The tick they found was *Dermacentor andersoni*, the Rocky Mountain wood tick. Steven Willett was murdered by Doctor Antonio Malandra. I'll bet my life on it."

"Oh! Good God! Are we going down that road again?" the chief roared. "Will you stop at nothing to vent your hatred of Tony Malandra?"

Bryce turned to Shopp. "Was his room secured?"

"No. You were right. The doors latch automatically of course, but the safety bar was not in place. The maid had no trouble getting in with her pass card around 10 a.m. He was lying on the bed, partially clothed. Time of death calculated to be around midnight. I called his brother. He was fine when he talked to him at around 9 p.m. He said he was up in Jacksonville trailing a suspect for the past few days. He didn't know much else."

"How long had he been in Florida?"

"Two weeks."

"It doesn't fit." Bryce turned to the chief. "I've been doing some research since I heard the news this morning. Even if it was the Australian tick, it was way too fast. That is the only tick that kills in a day. Tick paralysis in the Americas is caused by the dog tick and the Rocky Mountain wood tick, and they take several days to paralyze. If Willett had been in Florida for two weeks, how did he get a Rocky Mountain wood tick down there?" Bryce stared off into the mountains beyond the office windows. He stood there transfixed for several minutes.

Detective Shopp watched and waited quietly. Finally, Shopp's impatience got the best of him. "Doctor? What is it?"

Bryce turned slowly toward the officers, his focus not on them but out to infinity. "Do you remember what I told you about that old shed where Malandra kept the flesh-eating beetles? The one that so conveniently had a little fire when Bill's investigation began? He also had a jar of ticks in there. I saw it. Suppose a person kept a colony of *Dermacentor* alive by letting them feed on mammalian blood? Then took the adult females, the ones with the toxin in their saliva, and milked their mouth juices and concentrated it? It takes several days of prolonged feeding for a single female to kill a human since they only make a few nanograms of toxin per day. But if you collected multiple samples, combined them, got, say, a whole microgram of toxin and injected it, you would have a lethal dose. It could be very fast. And totally untraceable. Couple that with planting a live tick on the still-warm body where it would embed itself, and you have another perfect murder."

Chief Murphy threw his arms up in exasperation. "What kind of science-fiction mumbo jumbo are you talking about now? You need to let this go," he added as he plopped into his chair. "I swear if a meteor hit this building right now, you would blame it on Tony Malandra."

"You're scaring me, Doc," Shopp said. "Where do you guys come up with these ideas?"

"He's pushed me into a different realm, I will admit that. Bill told me I had to think like a crook to catch a crook. Told me I was too trusting. Well, no more."

"There is one more thing, Doc. I called the chief of detectives in Jacksonville and asked him to go immediately to Malandra's condo and question him. Establish an alibi, or lack thereof."

"And?"

"He's gone. Moved out yesterday. Walked out on his lease. Didn't even try to get his deposit back. No forwarding address. Nothing. Vanished."

Bryce slumped against the wall. "We are truly beaten then, aren't we? We'll never see him again. I lucked out finding him last time. Now who knows where he'll take off to? Is there any way you can do some deep dive, search FBI files, anything like that?"

"I can try," Shopp began but was interrupted by Chief Murphy's fist pounding the top of his desk.

"That's it. You are not wasting any more time on this bullshit, Shopp. Get back to your real investigations. Tony Malandra, a damn fine pathologist and a friend to the precinct, has been hounded out of town by all this crap, and I'm putting an end to this now. And I will thank you, Doctor Thompson, not to waste any more taxpayers' money on your crusade."

Bryce glared down at the chief as he walked to the front edge of the desk. "Then who killed my wife? And *two* of your detectives?"

"Oh, Christ! Bill collared so many guys in his twenty years on the force, it could have been any one out of a thousand."

"Anyone who had the knowledge and the laboratory capabilities to make a nerve gas and compress it into a tiny cylinder. Of course. Simple, right?" He turned away in disgust and walked over to Shopp. "Did Willett tell you about my trip to Florida? Did he tell you about the recording?"

"No. What recording?"

"I had a micro recorder on when I talked to Malandra. He as much as admitted his guilt. Willett didn't tell anyone about that? That was why he went to Florida."

"You went to Florida?" the Chief snarled. "You chased Tony all over this goddamn country?"

"How do you think Willett found him? You guys weren't doing your job. Someone had to. At least Willett believed me." Bryce turned back to Shopp. "Find out if there was any mention of a micro recorder camouflaged as a little black pen. It came with a pair of tiny headphones. Call your contact in Florida and tell him it's vital evidence, particularly if Willett got any of their conversation recorded in the motel room."

"I said this is over," the chief bellowed. "Now, get back to work, Shopp."

Bryce glared at the chief, then he turned and slammed the door as he strode to the parking lot, Shopp following in his wake. "I guess if you're going to break the law, you need to make friends at headquarters first. Thanks for trying, Detective." He shook Shopp's hand and went back to the clinic.

An hour later, Shopp called his cell phone. "No one found anything like that pen recorder or headphones in his hotel room or in his bags. I looked all over his office and nothing here either. Same with his wife and their home. I'm afraid whatever evidence you thought you had is gone."

"Well, at least you tried. Thanks."

35

BRYCE WAS WALKING TOWARD HIS WET BAR THAT EVENING when he looked out over the back yard and saw the gardens going to seed. The same gardens that Nicole had so lovingly planted, tended, and babied. Something jolted inside his temporal lobes. "I am ashamed of you, Bryce Thompson!" it said deep inside his brain. It was a mute voice screaming at him, and it was her voice. "Quit the pity party. Ditch the poor me attitude. That's what you always say. Don't give up. Never give up."

He walked to the bar, grabbed the Crown Royal, and dumped it down the drain, followed by the hundred-dollar Woodford Double Oaked. The rum and vodka followed. Then he changed into blue jeans and a T-shirt and attacked the gardens with a shovel and hoe. Feverishly pulling weeds and turning soil, sweat poured off him as if he had been hosed down. By the time full darkness descended on the valley, he had four 30-gallon trash barrels full of weeds and dead plants and three plastic tubs full of tomatoes, potatoes, and carrots he would drop off at the food bank in the morning.

He put four potatoes on to boil while he cleaned up. The shower felt awesome after his workout. He reveled in the hot water for several minutes longer than usual, trying to wash away the dirt along with the thick coat of self-pity that had been clinging to him like flies on a dung pile. Returning to the kitchen, he mashed the potatoes and coated them with melted butter, salt, and pepper, as near to the perfect meal as man has concocted when faced with little time and fewer resources. Exhausted, now maybe he could sleep. Maybe he would be too tired to dream. Maybe, without the alcohol, the dreams would fade.

But that hope would have to wait. Tossing in his sleep in the middle of the night, he could still hear Nicole's voice in his head. And then the dreams started once again. By morning, he was still unrested, and night after night, true rest eluded him. He would go for a run, trying to exhaust his muscles, trying to tire himself out so he could sleep, but nothing worked.

By the end of the week, he was tempted to take a sleeping pill, but he did not want to go down that rabbit hole. Friday night, the dream returned even more vividly. He was trapped on a window ledge, but this time it was Malandra's window ledge, not in New York but high in a black sky, no escape in sight. In the air, pieces of paper swirled about with nearly indistinguishable words scratched on them. It was all so meaningless. Then he saw it again. The tiny baby, faceless, crawling on ground littered with bones, crawling away into the bushes. He wanted to get to it, hold it, cherish it, but he was trapped. He tried to climb down from the window, and that was when he felt himself falling. Falling. Falling. Falling. That endless fall that haunts dreams seemed to last forever. He looked down into an abyss. The baby was gone. Everything was black. And then he smashed into the ground.

Bryce jolted awake. His head hurt. His arm was twisted underneath his torso. Disoriented, he tried to figure out where he was. He was lying in a heap on the floor, his head against the nightstand. He pulled himself up and walked to the bathroom, splashing cold water in his face, washing the sleep from his eyes. Heart racing, hyperventilating, he knew he was not going to be able to sleep. His head was swirling from the vividness of the dream. What was it that he had seen scrawled on those odd pieces of paper? Opium? Was that what he remembered from the dream? That was when it hit him. "Malandra's poem!" he said aloud as he staggered to his computer.

He pulled up the file and hit fast forward until he came to the pictures of the little office in the back of the house on Elm Street. He panned until he found the picture of the piece of paper tacked incongruously onto the wall. He enlarged the photo and read.

Xerxes in the cataracts,
opium in the pill.
Sad go the decades,
in which we all fall ill.
Deceased, forlorn cadaver.

What the hell does it mean? He read it over and over. *It's meaningless. What sense can I make out of that?* He sat and puzzled over it until the sun was warming the eastern horizon, and still he was no closer to an answer. He might as well have been reaching for that sunrise.

Bryce opened a word file to type it out and make a print copy. He typed the first line. Easy, because he had typed the word "cataracts" thousands of times when he recorded physical exam notes on elderly patients. He had always loved that word because you could reach with your right hand and take a sip of coffee, since cataracts was typed completely with the left hand. He began typing the second line. The word "opium" had been in his dream. Why? He finished typing and hit print but still had no clue as to the meaning.

By now, the sun was up, and he put on worn work clothes and did yard work, mowed, and then tried to read a medical journal. Half an hour later, he realized that the last thirty minutes were wasted. He could not recall a thing he read. His mind was elsewhere. He decided to go over to Bill's house and continue cleaning things out, preparing for an auction sale, the house no longer being sequestered as a crime scene.

At Bill's house, he went through the desk, drawer by drawer, saving anything with personal meaning, bagging the rest. He put all of Bill's pictures in boxes and loaded them into his pickup. He would go through them later, maybe when the pain would not cut as deep. He pulled a crib sheet from his wallet for the combination to Bill's little safe, squatted down in front of it, and twirled the dial. Fifty-seven left, twenty-three right, forty-nine left. Then Bryce jumped up and bolted to his pickup and raced to his house.

In the office, he opened the word file and began to type the poem out again. He came to the word "Opium," thinking that must be important, and that was when he realized that his left fingers were idle. Then the word "pill." All right fingers. He went back to "Xerxes"—all left hand. "Sad"—all left. "Go"—both hands. "The"—both. "Decades"— all left. "In"—all right hand. "Which"—both hands. "We"—all left. "Fall"—both. "Ill"—all right hand. "Deceased"—all left. "Forlorn"— both. "Cadaver"—all left. What was it that had hit him like a bolt of lightning at Bill's house? He sat back and looked at it. What was it?

Bryce stared at it, and a pattern began to emerge. The first and last words of each sentence were typed with the same hand. He glanced back at the picture of the paper stuck to the wall. That was when he saw it. Malandra Dry Cleaning. The huge black safe.

"It's a combination!" he thundered.

He began counting. Left hand, Xerxes, 6 letters. Cataracts, 9 letters. Right hand, Opium, 5 letters. Pill, 4 letters. Left hand, sad, 3 letters, decades, 7 letters. In, 2 letters. Ill, 3 letters. Deceased, 8 letters. Cadaver, 7 letters. He jotted them down in the right margin.

Xerxes in the cataracts,	L69
opium in the pill.	R54
Sad go the decades,	L37
in which we all fall ill.	R23
Deceased, forlorn cadaver.	L87

Bryce looked at the safe in the picture with the faded white lettering. Malandra Dry Cleaning. He read it out loud even as Nicole's voice echoed in his head, "Never give up." And, before he had finished, he knew he was heading back to New York.

36

B RYCE PULLED THE RENTAL CAR AGAINST THE CURB AND PARKED in front of 110 Elm Street. Back in Hudson Falls, he was certain that Tony Malandra would not be here this time. He even wondered if Francis Malandra would still be here, or if the loving son would relocate her, too. Unlikely, knowing how elderly people hate change. He walked to the front door and knocked several times. He could hear movement inside, and soon a gray-haired lady looked out through the clear glass pane, studying him. He held up Bill's badge and spoke loudly.

"Police."

She unlocked and opened the door, her frightened look impossible to miss. "What is it, Officer?"

"I am looking for a man named Antonio Malandra. Do you know his whereabouts?"

"No. I haven't heard from him in weeks. Is he in trouble?"

"We don't know yet. We just have some questions for him. Some unfinished business back in Montana. We can't seem to locate him. He was last seen in Florida, but then he disappeared. Are you sure you haven't heard from him? He told his coworkers you were ill. We know he was here a few weeks ago."

"I haven't been ill. He just came to visit. Then he left in the middle of the night without saying goodbye. I knew something must have been wrong."

"Did you know he had a place in Florida?"

"No. He never mentioned that."

"He is a friend to us at the precinct, and we are concerned about his well-being. Do you know if he has any other property where he could be staying, like a lake cabin or a beach resort where he can get away and relax?"

"No, sir. Tony is a very private person. He doesn't talk much about his private business."

"I have a search warrant to look around the premises," he said, waving a small sheaf of papers he had printed off his computer that looked very official. "I won't be long, but I need to look around."

Like most people of her generation, Francis Malandra was obsequious when it came to authority figures and didn't hesitate when Bryce asked her to sign the acknowledgment page of his purported search warrant. He entered the house and began looking around. He feigned interest in the pictures on the walls but soon headed for the little office in the back corner of the house, the little office that held such frightful memories. He loitered around the desk, then turned to Mrs. Malandra. "I need to call my Captain. Do you mind if I close this door? It's a private matter."

"No. Of course not, Officer," she said as she went back to her kitchen.

Bryce shut the door, put on vinyl gloves, and went through all the desk drawers. Nothing. Then he went to the safe. *If I have any chance of finding him, it's inside these steel walls.* He swirled the dial to the left a half dozen times, picking up all the tumblers, then turned left to 69, then right three times to 54, left to 37 twice, and, holding his breath, he turned it once to the right to 23 and felt the tumblers clunk into place. He slowly turned left to 87 and could feel the resistance of the bolts sliding out of their recesses. He pulled, and the massive door swung open, shedding light on the dark life of Doctor Antonio Malandra.

37

THE STACKS OF HUNDRED-DOLLAR BILLS, EACH BUNDLE OF A hundred bills neatly collated and banded, were impossible to miss, stashed here and there between gold-plated pistols and dozens upon dozens of plastic containers, each one housing twenty Krugerrands, American Eagles, Austrian Philharmonics, or Australian Kangaroos, and the cream of the crop for international investors—specially-struck Canadian Maple Leafs, 0.99999 gold content.

Bryce had never seen so much money in one place. He stood and stared in disbelief for several seconds, but it wasn't money he was interested in. He immediately grabbed the accordion folders and began rifling through them. It took only a few minutes to hit pay dirt. He grabbed the property title to the house on Providence Island, Nassau, Bahamas, snapped several pictures of each page and focused in on the map and the picture of the house. It was nestled in an oversized lot with plenty of trees affording privacy off of Twynam Heights Boulevard, close to Winton Beach and not far from downtown and the marinas.

Almost unnoticed, he picked up a 5" x 8" note card with names on it, and to the right of each name were numbers. It would have been unnoticed, except Bryce knew the names too well, particularly the last one. Zebrowski -----5.0-----2.5

Bryce knew immediately what he was looking at. An insecure hunter, obsessed with his trophies and whose ego is up on the wall, needs a record of his accomplishments, and Tony Malandra was at the apex of the hunter-collector breed. He needed a record, a trophy, and here it was. Bryce knew each of these names because Bill had handed him their medical records, and Bryce had pored over them for hours that spring and summer. Mrs. Zebrowski had collected five million dollars in insurance money, and Bryce was holding a list of Malandra's conquests, a summary of the source of his wealth, his fifty percent share, on a small white note card, the biggest trophy of them all. He loaded pictures of the cash bundles, the gold coins, and the 5" x 8" note card in a file and sent them to his home computer. Some day he intended to show that stack of pictures to Chief Murphy and ask him to kindly shove it where the sun doesn't shine.

Well before he had finished snapping pictures, a plan was forming in Bryce Thompson's brain. Next stop—the Bahamas. He pocketed the note card and one bundle of bills for travel expenses, then closed the safe's door and twirled the dial on Hudson Falls, New York.

38

T HE THUMP OF THE LANDING GEAR LOCKING INTO PLACE WAS barely noticed as Bryce gazed out the window, getting his bearings above Nassau, the maps long since locked into his long-term memory banks. Upon landing, he gathered his bags and headed for the rental car desk, where he signed out the largest SUV in their inventory. There was no need to use an alias now. He was no longer under the eye of U.S. law.

After checking in at his hotel, Bryce spent the next few hours driving around the island, first to reconnoiter Malandra's property, then orienting himself to the city and the island, finding the shops he would need as a makeshift plan began to congeal in his brain. At the fishing supply shop, he bought eight feet of one-ton-test fish netting and a large roll of quarter-inch floating poly. Other various supplies slowly filled his SUV, and by sundown, he was equipped and settled into his rooms.

Sunrise found Bryce parked on the south side of Twynam Heights Boulevard, the brilliant Bahamian sun shining on Malandra's getaway, illuminating Bryce's next obstacle. Did Malandra have cameras? Would he install them? Did he think he needed them down here? Only time would tell.

At midmorning, a car pulled out of the garage, a single male driver speeding away in an impeccably restored 1955 Peugeot 203 convertible. Bryce put on his wraparound sunglasses, gray beard, and ponytail hat and limped casually up and down the sidewalks as he studied the heavily wooded property, by far the largest on the block, with privacy afforded by its isolation as well as the lush foliage providing shade and secrecy to one who needed it. Satisfied that he knew the layout, Bryce sauntered onto the property, searching for cameras but finding none. They were either well hidden, the new micro cameras that look like a part of the building, or Malandra hadn't taken the time to install them yet. He could only hope for the latter.

He strolled nonchalantly around to the back yard and saw immediately why Malandra might not need cameras. A long dog run attached to the house held two massive Great Danes, their snarling noses pressed against the chain-link kennel. They obviously did not like strangers encroaching on their territory. They had access to food, water, and shade, but they also had access to the inside of the house via a spring-loaded kennel door. The Danes were a great deterrent for Saturday-night burglars but not good enough.

Bryce finished his appraisal of the property, then headed to the island's only big box home improvement store. He purchased a handful of O-ring lags, two twelve-foot closet rods, several bungee cords, and various tools. Now he just had to wait for his next opportunity.

After watching the house from a distance for two days, Bryce's opportunity came when he saw Malandra loading scuba gear into a Jeep inside his open garage early that morning, then speeding away.

He couldn't have asked for a better setup. A scuba diving outing would give him several hours to get ready. He started his SUV and followed Malandra at a discrete distance. He needed to be sure that he was not going to return home soon. Once he saw Malandra unloading his gear and carting it to a dive boat, he drove back to Twynam and pulled into the driveway.

First order of business was grabbing a bag from his front seat and walking around to the back of the house. He could hear a low, menacing growl even before he rounded the back corner and approached the kennel. Walking to the far end of the dog run, away from the dog door, he began tossing small pieces of freshly cut meat into the kennel. Speaking softly, he coaxed the dogs closer. "Come," he said gently. "Good boy. Good boy," he repeated as the first one caught scent of the fresh beef. Soon, both dogs were following him, gulping up the steak bites in the usual dog fashion, one chew and one gulp and looking for more. Once they were calm and sniffing at his fingers through the chain-links, getting to know his scent, he hurried back to the SUV and grabbed the closet rods from the roof rack and carried them to the back of the house. He distracted the dogs once more with two pieces of roast that were too big to gulp quickly, throwing them to the far end of the run. As the dogs hurried to the meat, Bryce slid the curtain rods through the chain-link fence holes at the top and bottom of the kennel door and through corresponding holes in the opposite side of the fence, locking the dogs out of the house.

Retrieving his tool bag, he went to the far side of the house where he was concealed from prying eyes in the foliage. He grasped the glass cutter and cut a nearly perfect circle in the window, just above the latch. Using the metal ball on the base of the glass cutter, he tapped the etched circle systematically around its entire perimeter, creating full-thickness fracture lines through the glass. Next, he attached a suction cup to the center of the circle and pulled as he continued to tap the perimeter, finishing the fracture lines and popping the circle of glass clear of the pane. Bryce reached in and unlocked the window, raised the lower sash, and crawled inside. For an instant, he felt like he was back in New York. *I've seen this movie before.*

He used two-inch clear tape to replace the circle of glass and then began his exploration of the house. It was a one-story structure with a fairly typical layout, and he made his way through to the kennel door. He drove two self-tapping screws through the corners of the door and into the stud behind. Next, he went out through the garage door and removed the wooden rods and secured them once again to the vehicle's roof rack. Now, if Malandra checked on the dogs from the back yard, he would see nothing out of the ordinary. Tasks completed, Bryce moved his vehicle down the block and parked it out of sight around the curve in the street, gathered the rest of his gear, and hurried back to the house.

When he had surveyed Malandra's activities, Malandra had always left the premises in a vehicle via the garage, so Bryce was quite confident that would be the door he would use on reentering the house. He took six eye lag bolts and screwed them into the ceiling above the walk-in door from the garage, two rows of three, then threaded two lengths of rope through the eyes and secured them loosely with a slipknot. He then threaded another rope through the lower perimeter of the fish netting and clipped this to the ceiling rope with mini carabiners so it would slide easily. Bryce tied several lead fishing weights to this lower perimeter of the fish netting, ensuring it would fall quickly. With plenty of rope, he could control his contraption from across the room. He readied his other equipment, then tied the rope with a slipknot to the chair in the dark corner opposite the door. To ensure that Malandra would enter through the booby-trapped door, he drove a screw through the corner of the front door, locking it into the frame.

Now he had time to study the house in more depth. The living room was pedestrian, as was the dining and kitchen area, and the first two bedrooms were standard. But when he walked into the largest bedroom at the back of the house, he knew instantly what Malandra used this room for. There was a double-sized foam mattress on the floor against the largest wall covered with white cotton sheets and a dozen pillows scattered around. Sex toys and scented body oils graced the bedside stands.

A sliding glass door led to a patio with a large hot tub nestled under the trees. Bryce made sure that this door opened easily in case he had to make a hasty retreat. Oriented to his new surroundings, he went back to the front room, unscrewed the light bulbs in the ceiling fixture, took his chair in the corner of the room, and began his long wait.

Although each minute seemed to take a thousand seconds to tick by, this is what Bryce had come for, and he had all the time in the world. Time was all he had. Everything else had been taken from him. He could handle this, no matter how long he had to wait. Dusk had seeped between the base of the trees, and the moon had climbed halfway up the tree limbs when he heard the automatic garage door opener whirring and a vehicle pulling into the garage. He loosened the slipknot and held the long rope in his right hand.

The garage door clanged shut, and footsteps approached the doorway. The door creaked slightly as it swung into the garage, and a hand reached for the light switch. "Shit! Now what?" Malandra grunted when the lights failed to work. He closed the door behind him, and life as he knew it changed in that second. Bryce pulled the rope through the carabiners, releasing the net as he bounded from the chair and was at Malandra's side in three strides. Malandra was completely enmeshed in the fishing net, and the more he struggled, the worse it became. Bryce pulled on the rope threaded through the bottom of the netting, tightening it around Malandra's legs, then sent him to the ground with a smashing fist to the jaw.

"That was for Steven Willett, you son of a bitch. He had a wife and three kids, not that you would care."

"You can't prove a thing," Malandra stammered, confused and still trying to figure out what had happened.

Bryce screwed the light bulbs back into their sockets. "Let there be light," he intoned, "and behold, there was light."

"You are one crazy son of a bitch, Thompson," Malandra said, his eyes darting, trying to figure out an escape plan. "I suppose it's another trip back to Montana."

"Doubtful," Bryce replied. "There was no justice there, just legalities."

"Then what did you come here for?"

"I came here for the justice that eluded me in Montana."

Malandra gave him a prolonged stare. "But I can see the doubt in your eyes. You don't believe in the death penalty. You don't believe any man has the right to take another man's life. I remember those conversations like they were yesterday. You believe in saving life, preserving life. You took an oath, and you have lived by that oath."

"Unlike you."

"Look, Thompson, I'm no saint. But you? You keep your word. You live by some code I can't understand, even when it puts you at such a disadvantage. That's why everyone respects you."

"Just a few weeks ago, you were telling me how stupid I was and how brilliant you were. Now that I control your fate, I'm suddenly looked up to. Tony, if you told me the sun was setting in the west, I would have to go and look for myself."

"Seriously, I meant it. I thought that little detour to Florida would throw you off. I don't know how you did it, but you figured it out. You outsmarted me, Bryce. I'll admit it. That's why everyone looks up to you, whether you know it or not. You work your ass off, you do free care for those in need, you never raise your voice even when a code is going south, the nurses think you walk on water, and administration wishes they could clone you. What's not to respect?"

"Enough of your bullshit. I have work to do," Bryce added as he walked over to the crumpled pile in front of the door and stabbed a needle into Malandra's right gluteus. "Good night, Tony," he said as he buried the plunger.

By the time Bryce walked to the kitchen and drank a glass of water, Tony Malandra was sliding into another drug-induced sleep.

39

WHEN MALANDRA AWAKENED, GOLDEN SUNLIGHT WAS JUST peeking through a partially opened curtain. "What the hell?" he blurted as he tried to move his arms.

"Good morning, Tony. Sleep well?" Bryce was sitting in the corner chair, sipping a cup of fresh coffee.

Malandra looked down at his wrists strapped to the arms of a chair and then at his naked legs strapped to the legs of the chair. He looked at his naked bottom and realized he had only a T-shirt on. He glared at Bryce. "A bedside commode? Seriously?"

"It's better than you deserve, Tony. I could have just let you crap your pants and stew in it." He took another sip of coffee. "This way, you can just go whenever you feel the need."

"I thought I would be dead by now."

"As did I."

"You can't do it, can you? That code is too strong in you."

"I don't know what I can and can't do. I'm still trying to figure that out. But first, I want to figure you out. What is it that lets you do what you do? Why do you do it? Is it the money? If a million dollars isn't enough, if five million dollars isn't enough, how much is enough?"

"Money is freedom, Bryce. Money is power. Money is the ticket to this world. Money is the only thing humans understand. Let them spew their lofty platitudes, but in the end, money is their true deity."

"Sorry. I can't be quite that cynical."

"Why do you think that every politician who goes to Congress with the best of intentions ends up groveling for the dollar? And they all come out of Congress wealthy. Just like a body needs food and water to survive, the human brain needs power and authority to feel fulfilled. All the feel-good bullshit in the world can't hold a candle to the power of gold."

"It's all about power to you, isn't it? Power is your aphrodisiac, isn't it?"

"It doesn't hurt, but it's more than that. The world is controlled by the powerful. And the powerful have money. That's why the system is rigged. You can blather on about social justice and voting equality all you want, but money controls it all. Hell, ninety percent of the population has no clue what the issues are. They vote for reasons they don't even understand. They're too lazy to do their own research and too stupid to realize they've been manipulated. That's why there will be poor always, and you and I can get rich."

"Money only buys you stuff. It will never buy you love, happiness, or fulfillment."

"More platitudes."

Bryce got up, went to the kitchen, and brewed another cup of coffee. He ambled back into the living room and pulled the drapes open a few inches, staring out at the sun rising over the ocean.

"What do you want, Bryce? I'm still alive, so I know you want more than to just kill me."

"I want justice. I want you to pay for taking my family from me. You should be rotting in a prison in Montana, but the system didn't want to hear my half of the story. They just wanted to assure you of your rights."

"Just proves I'm right. Again."

"How so?"

"The county attorney, Ms. Goodwin? She wants to be a senator. And Chief Murphy? He wants to be mayor when he retires from the force, maybe move on to higher office. But the Bryce Thompsons of the world don't pay attention to that social trivia. You have no clue about their aspirations. Thus, you don't understand that a few envelopes, a few thousand here, a few thousand there, given in confidence to "help out our cause" by the model citizen who does their autopsies and helps them win their cases, bend their mind without them even knowing it. Subconsciously, they trust me, and they don't know you. They can't help it. They see you as the overly distraught widower and me as the victim of your zeal. And good luck with extradition. I've made sure to befriend the governor down here with some nice contributions for his reelection over the past couple of years. We're on a first-name basis. Bryce, real power isn't a frontal assault. Real power is in the undercurrent. You just have to know how to shape the wiring."

"Your view of man is very warped, Tony."

"My view of man is exactly what I see! What I work with! You're the one looking through rose-tinted lenses. Man is cheap and cruel and low and will do whatever he needs to do to get ahead. Man is no different than any other animal. He will fight and kill to win, to survive."

"That's it? That's your entire view of man? Just another animal trying to survive in this cruel world?"

"The facts speak for themselves. Animals need food, water, shelter, and procreation. Their genes are coded for it. And often, man will sacrifice the first three for number four. Just look at man's behavior worldwide. We are more a victim of our genes than anyone wants to admit. And that is why those who understand are the ones with the money and the power. We are the ones who don't let platitudes get in the way. There is no god, no heaven, no hell. The masses are lulled by the hollow promise of religion and a better life yet to come. Religion! The true combination drug. Opiate and benzo rolled into one, rendering the masses compliant to the ruling class."

"That is your definition of success? How sad for you." Bryce got up and poured another cup of coffee. He paced around the room for a couple of minutes, lost in thought, then returned to his seat. "I don't know what to do with you yet, but I do want one thing. I want you to admit, beyond a shadow of a doubt, that you are guilty. That you killed my family. That you killed them in the most cold-blooded way imaginable. I want you to admit that."

"You said it. You figured me out."

"No! Bill figured you out. He was the one who understood scum like you. I wrote down all the evidence, but I failed to see the connection. I was still wearing those rose-tinted glasses. But no more."

"So, you are admitting I was right about man."

"Don't change the subject. Admit your guilt."

"Goddammit Bryce! How could I have known he was your brother? And how in the hell could I have possibly known your wife would be there that few seconds of that day? What are the odds?"

"Admit it! You killed them in cold blood!"

"I wouldn't have done it if I had known it was your family. You have to believe that."

"Quit dancing around the question. They wouldn't let me depose you under oath in Montana, so admit it now. I want to hear you say it."

"What difference does it make? You're going to kill me anyway."

"Say it! I want to hear you say it. I want there to be no doubt. No matter what I decide, I want no doubt lurking in the recesses of my brain to haunt me with dreams in the middle of the night for the rest of my life. I want closure. I need closure."

"Look, Bryce. I can make you rich beyond your wildest dreams. Let me live, and I can make you an instant multimillionaire. I'll buy my life with everything I have. You'll never have to work again."

"Quit dodging. Admit it!"

"Twenty million. Is that enough to buy my life?"

"Admit it!"

"OK. I killed them. Are you satisfied? But your wife was an accident. I would never have done it if I had known he was your brother and never, never would have dreamed of it if I had known she would be there. You have to give me that much benefit of the doubt."

"I don't have to give you shit." Bryce stormed out of the house and walked to the end of the street, letting the culmination of his quest sink in. He knew Malandra was guilty, had known it all along, but he was surprised at the effect it had on him, hearing it from Malandra's own lips, not a shred of doubt lingering. His anger had been pent up for weeks, and now it exploded inside him, leaving him trembling with rage, unable to focus. He wanted to smash something. Instead, he broke into a run, trying to disseminate the adrenaline. He sprinted to the end of the street, then turned and ran back again to the opposite end of the curving road, again and again, until he was drenched with sweat, his kindled wrath blazing into full fury as he burned through his pent-up emotions. Exhausted, he returned to the house and cooled down with a long shower.

After he dressed, he poured himself a Coke on ice, then mixed an extra-strong whiskey coke and walked back to the front room. "I heard this is your favorite," he said as he offered it to Malandra through a straw. "Enjoy!"

Malandra took several long gulps, savoring the taste and the numbing sting of the alcohol. Bryce set the drink on the end table next to Malandra and returned to his chair.

"Thanks, Bryce. I needed that." He paused as he looked Bryce in the eye. "You see, that's what I mean about you. That's why everyone looks up to you. Anyone else would have smashed my face in, beat me until I bled to death. Stabbed or shot me. But you—you fix me a drink. Everyone looks at me and sees money and success. They look at you and see the person they want to emulate."

Bryce looked at Tony but didn't say a word, lost more in thought than present in the moment.

Malandra went on. "I meant what I said, Bryce. I can make you very rich. Very, very rich. I can give you the means to buy whatever you want. Go wherever you want. Do whatever you want, whenever you want. I'll trade my millions for my life. You're a man of your word, Bryce. I would trust you to keep your end of the bargain."

Still, there was no response from across the room.

Malandra sat for another minute, waiting, then went on. "I have the money in two numbered accounts in Switzerland. I will give you the numbers and the passwords, and you can have the money transferred here. You'll be independent. You can do whatever you want."

"What do you use it for, Tony?" Bryce took a sip of his cola. "What does it do for you?"

"Okay. You want details." He glanced down at the drink. "Can I have a little more of that?"

Bryce walked over and cut the plastic tie from Malandra's left wrist, then returned to his seat.

Malandra took several long gulps of the drink, then looked back across the room. "Travel abroad, scuba diving, sailing, flying, skydiving. The best meals, the finest wines, five-star restaurants. That's all fun, but the parties are the best. When you have money, the parties just flow. Everyone wants to be your friend, especially in a place like this, where there are so many poor girls. They practically beg to be invited. Spread the money around, and they'll do anything you want to win your favor. And I mean anything. The sex waxes like a high tide, and you can't get enough." He finished his drink and held it out to Bryce, begging for more with his eyes.

Bryce refilled it, stronger, then sat again. "Go on."

"Have you ever had three or four at once? All of them legal, sixteen, with perfect bodies, vying to please you? Or if it's what you like, a friend will bring you a fourteen-year-old. Or even thirteen. Let's admit it. The forbidden attracts us. That alone is enough to crank up the libido, but then you add in a couple of drinks and a half jolt of Ecstasy, and the orgasms are out of this world." He took another long pull on his drink, the flush glowing on his neck. "And Bryce, you're actually doing them a favor. When you tip them an extra hundred or two, you just bought food for their family for a week. Left to their own devices, they would be pulling tricks for a twenty, happy to get it. Just like anything else in life, it's give and take, and if both parties benefit, where's the harm?" He took another drink, his tongue loosening as the ethanol worked its magic. "Look at all the good you could do with that money."

"Let's talk about that money, Tony. How you got it. How you went about it. I think I know, but I want to be sure. I know Zebrowski was a combination of alcohol and cocaine, but how could you be sure it would kill him and not just knock him out for several hours?"

"Ah! You leave nothing to chance. After he's out cold, the concentrated solution of potassium chloride stops the heart. Undetectable on blood tests. You just have to inject it so no one sees the mark. Of course, if you can get the autopsy assigned to your list and not sent to the state ME, then it's a cakewalk."

"And how did you get their spouses to go along with it? Weren't they afraid of discovery? Of consequences?"

"You do your research and pick carefully. They were all cheating or doing something illegal. After I told the spouse to be out of town with an airtight alibi, they were more than happy to get rid of the cheating bums. Again, it just proves I'm right about the human condition."

"And the money? How could you be sure they would pay up?"

"That was easy enough. My contact was always by phone, always anonymous. They never saw my face. I reminded them that I knew them, but they didn't know me. I could always find them if they didn't pay. Scared the hell out of them. All they had to do was make a bank transfer to Switzerland when they got the insurance check, and they would never hear from me again. It was perfect, until you screwed it up."

"How about Swenson? I'm guessing a huge bolus of Heparin during the evening of the night he died?"

"You're good. Two for two. What a piece of cake when they are an inpatient in the very hospital where you work. Just had to make sure the wife arranged it so our hospital got the case."

"And Corsello? Insulin overdose late in the evening?"

"You're on a roll." Malandra laughed as he took another swig of the whiskey. "Easy enough. Just stroll up onto the ward during a rapid response at the other end of the hall. A rapid response that I called," he chuckled. "Takes all of five seconds, then quickly back down to the department. If anyone asks, the techs can swear I was down there all night working on slides."

"How about Bancroft? Congestive heart failure, pulmonary edema, followed by sudden cardiac death. Cardiac arrhythmia from dig toxicity? The loving wife taught how to sprinkle five hundred micrograms into his food each evening?"

"A thousand." Malandra laughed and took another drink. "Didn't want to piss around with small doses and risk him getting sick and diagnosed by some smart doctor. We started it right after his annual checkup when he had perfectly normal blood panels. That way, no one suspected dig toxicity. He didn't suffer. The arrhythmia took him out quickly. None of them suffered, in fact."

"You say that as if you cared," Bryce sneered.

"Well, they didn't."

"How about Jensen? I wouldn't call flying off the highway on his Roadster at sixty miles an hour painless."

"What made you think I had anything to do with that?"

"A four-million-dollar life insurance policy, a twenty-two-year-old girlfriend, and a pissed-off forty-eight-year-old wife. It had your name written all over it."

Malandra smiled as he finished the drink. "Dumb ass took off without a helmet. Smashed his head on a rock when he left the road after I bumped him. He died instantly. I stopped and made sure before I headed back home."

"There was another case I came across that had your finger-prints on it, but I wasn't sure. The Emerson case. Elderly male, died of overwhelming sepsis after developing agranulocytosis, six million in insurance, young trophy wife. He was reported to be going crazy, then died very quickly when his white blood count fell from five thousand to less than two hundred. What happened there?"

"Ever use clozapine?"

"Nope. Never bothered to get clearance. I left that to the psych squad."

"Smart of you. It works great for some psychotics, but it can wipe out the white blood cells, specifically the neutrophils. And if they don't know they are getting it, they are not getting their weekly blood counts. He conveniently had prostate problems and recurrent urinary tract infections. As he became more and more sedated from the high doses, she just made excuses to the few friends who asked about him, then took him to the hospital when he collapsed with infection. The whole thing was witnessed and documented that he died of sepsis and idiopathic neutropenia due to old age. I made three on that one alone, but it was so beautiful, I should have charged her four."

Bryce got up and refilled their glasses, then paced the floor for several minutes. "I hate to admit this, Tony, but you've got me thinking. Suppose I do let you live. How do I get the money?"

"It's pretty easy. First you go to one of the bigger banks on the island and open an account with cash. Make sure you work with the president of the bank himself. Then tip him a couple of hundred in cash for his 'personal attention' and make him think you're his newest best friend. And you will be his newest best friend if you tip him every time for his trouble. Then you open an account with a safe deposit box and a regular checking account and give him the number to the Swiss account. He will enter the number, then you will tap in the passwords and have a few thousand in cash transferred to make sure it all works right. Put most of the cash in the box and slip him a couple hundred again. Let him watch you deposit the cash so he knows you're not doing some quick drug deal, then start moving the money from Switzerland into your new account, taking enough cash each time to stay below the reporting limits but plenty to live on. If you never try to get large sums into the U.S., no one cares. Eventually, you'll have millions transferred, and he will greet you at the door personally when you call ahead to make an appointment. Like I said, money is the great lubricant of human transactions." Malandra laughed and took another drink.

"You make it sound too easy. There has to be a catch," Bryce said as he paced the room.

"Not as long as you act confident and in charge. Act suspicious, and they will view you as suspicious."

Bryce took another drink of his cola and continued to pace, lost in thought. After a couple of minutes, Malandra spoke again.

"What have you got to lose? Go downtown and give it a try. Just a few thousand, keep it under ten, to test the system. You'll see I'm not trying to con you. Prove for yourself that it works. You get your money, and we can part ways."

"Only to have you hunt me down and kill me? Some day, some place, some time, always looking over my shoulder, always wondering when you will show up to finish the job? What a life that would be."

"I swear, Bryce. I know you don't trust me, but I trust you. If you get the money, you will let me live. Your word is your bond. But

I swear on my mother's honor that I will not hunt you down or try to harm you in any way. You've bested me, and I accept it."

"Give me the numbers. And the passwords. I'll make a trial run."

"Get a paper and pencil. It's a lot of numbers. I have them memorized. Something that important makes it easy to memorize." He dictated the account numbers and passwords as Bryce jotted them down and read them back. "It's a go," he added as Bryce read the last digits. "Now we can get this over with and get on with the rest of our lives."

Malandra drained his drink as Bryce left the room, then came back in with a syringe in hand. "Oh crap. Not another nap?"

"Sorry. Protocol demands it," Bryce said as he injected the medication into Malandra's right buttock, exposed as it was on the commode. "Sleep tight, Tony. Five of Haldol and five of Valium on top of three strong drinks guarantees I'll have all day to do my banking and shopping without having to worry about you escaping."

"Five of each? I'll be lucky to be breathing."

"You're pretty lucky. I wouldn't worry about it too much. I've learned your tolerance over the past couple of months."

Bryce placed a fresh zip tie around Malandra's left wrist, securing it to the arm of the chair. He removed the screw and taped a note to the front door saying Malandra had gone diving until Monday, just in case one of his great friends came by with a thirteen-year-old who needed a favor. He rifled through Malandra's things until he found the key to the front door, then headed to his hotel and changed into business casual. First stop, the bank, then shopping for the next few days' plans, plans that were still forming in Bryce's head.

A quick Internet search revealed over 250 banks licensed in the Bahamas, many affiliated with or having home offices in other countries. It took less than a minute to key in on Credit Suisse, with offices in the local financial center plaza downtown as well as Zurich. He headed to Charlotte Street, between Bay and Shirley. Bryce was pleasantly surprised at how quickly it all went, exactly like Malandra had explained it. The bank president was delighted with his new customer, and the transfer of thousands of dollars was uneventful, obviously not a novelty in this offshore establishment.

The rest of the day was spent shopping for camping supplies, tents, cookstoves, dry goods, nonperishable foodstuffs, freeze-dried meals, as well as medical equipment and medications. It was past dark by the time he returned to Malandra's house, where he fed the dogs and filled their water containers. Malandra was still in a deep sleep, and Bryce got his first good night's sleep in weeks. The following morning, he fed Tony and then gave him half the dose of the previous day before heading out to finish his shopping. A quick stop at the bank and another larger money transfer with the help of his newest best friend went off without a hitch.

After a trip to the home improvement store for a few odds and ends and another stop at the medical supply store for more medicinals, easy enough with his AMA card, his shopping was complete. He stopped back at the bank late that afternoon and was ushered into the president's office.

"Gabriel," he said as he took the hand of the bank president in an extended grasp, "I need another favor. I see on the web there are some islands for sale. Could you possibly help me with a transaction?"

If the smile wasn't large enough, the wide-eyed expression on the face of the bank president belied the math taking place in his head as he calculated the real estate fees he would net on a million-dollar deal. "Of course, I would be only too happy to help, Mister Thompson."

The next hour saw the paperwork completed, two million transferred, and Bryce holding the title to his own private island. It was a small oasis of white sand and sparse green growth in the southern portion of the chain of seven hundred islands known as the Commonwealth of The Bahamas. "Now, there is one more thing," Bryce said as he placed the papers in a large manila envelope. "I need a boat. A very large boat with a large open area in the back for supplies, twin engines, and extra-large fuel tanks."

The bank president picked up his phone and dialed a number. "Jonathon, my friend. This is Gabriel. Please do not leave work yet. I am going to drive a very special friend over to your shop. He needs your personal attention. Trust me, it will be worth your time."

After a short drive to the harbor, they walked into the largest boat dealership on the island, the owner beaming as the bank president introduced Bryce. Thirty minutes later, Bryce signed the purchase agreement on the beautiful Luhrs 41-foot cabin cruiser with 660 horsepower twin diesel engines, while the banker completed the cashier's check for just over $600,000.

"Thank you so much," the dealership owner said. "Is there anything else I can do for you?"

"Yes. Tomorrow, I would like a personal demonstration and test run. The day after tomorrow, I will need four strong men to help me load heavy gear onto the boat. Also, I want them to bring thirty, no, make that forty, five-gallon fuel canisters of premium diesel to the boat after they top off the tanks. That should be all. Thank you so much," Bryce added as he extended a warm handshake. "You have been so helpful."

The bank president drove Bryce back to his vehicle and bid him good day. "If there is anything else you need, please do not hesitate to ask. I look forward to a long relationship."

"Believe me, I know who to call if I need anything. You have been most helpful," Bryce said as he shook his hand. "I'll be in touch." He started to walk toward his rental, then abruptly turned back. "Actually, there is one more thing. I need the name of a dog shelter. I cannot take my dogs where I am going. I need them picked up first thing in the morning. Two dogs. Two very large dogs." He jotted down the address and handed it to the bank president.

"I will take care of it personally," the banker promised.

Malandra was still groggy when Bryce returned to the house, so Bryce took a long, hot shower and then made a large pan of ahi and udon noodles with fish sauce.

"Rise and shine, Sleeping Beauty," he called out as he brought a huge plate of food to the end table on Malandra's left. Bryce clipped the tie from his left arm again and handed him a plastic fork. "Need to keep your strength up. We still have a lot to accomplish."

"How did the bank run go?" Malandra asked as he devoured the food.

"Seamless. Just like you said, Tony," Bryce answered as he dug into his own bowl of noodles. "You were right again."

"So, we have a deal!" Malandra said, trying not to sound triumphant. "You get your payday, and I buy my life. We both start over."

"I guess you're right again," he mumbled through his noodles. "Tomorrow is a new day and the start of a new life. In the back of my mind, I have always thought it would be rewarding to go somewhere and care for the poor while I see the world. Somewhere where you could never find me. I have nothing to keep me here, and I can afford it now."

"That is so you, Bryce. You always see the positive aspect of any situation. You take lemons and make lemonade."

40

"SHE HANDLES LIKE A DREAM," BRYCE HOLLERED AS HE TURNED a full-throttle 360 in the open waters north of the island, his hair flattened back on his scalp by the blast of oncoming air up in the flybridge. "You never have the feeling that she will capsize, even at these speeds."

"Exactly why we handle the Luhrs," the instructor answered. "Their wide beam makes them stable, perfect for rough seas, and they have a great setup for fishing. Plus, she has the comfortable interior, large sleeping cabin, shower, stove, fridge, 600 gallons of diesel, 130-gallon fresh-water tank, the works. You can stay out for weeks in this sweetheart and not feel claustrophobic. You pay for a little more drag, but the keel design and ballast are worth every penny in rough seas. There are many souls at the bottom of this ocean who were penny wise and pound foolish," he shouted, his Bahamian accent revealing pride in his knowledge of English literature.

"I love it. Perfect for my needs," Bryce shouted against the onslaught of air as he straightened her out and headed back toward the harbor. "And the GPS is so intuitive, it's like reading a road map."

"And her name?" the instructor shouted back. "You want that painted on the transom when we get back?"

"Yes. Justice Cay," Bryce said as he guided the boat back into the harbor.

The following morning, four massively built islanders arrived at the house at dawn and began loading their van and flatbed trailer with the goods Bryce had laid out in the front room. "Be especially careful with that large tent," he cautioned as he handed the leader a wad of hundred-dollar bills. "It has many boxes of wine packed inside, and it is very heavy. Wouldn't want to lose the wine, now, would we?" he chuckled as they all made horrific faces at that thought. The process was repeated at the boat dock, the supplies packed carefully in the cabin, the fore and aft decks overflowing with fuel canisters and camping and fishing gear. As the blazing Bahamian sun approached its noon apogee, Bryce was on his way to his very own private island one hundred miles to the southeast. He cruised at a comfortable 20 knots, the 660 horsepower diesels capable of more but at the expense of inefficient fuel burn.

About halfway there, he pulled into a small harbor on one of the inhabited islands and topped off the fuel tanks, saving the cached fuel for later. As the sun coursed beyond the westering clouds, its golden light giving way to evening red, the GPS guided him into the leeward side of his little island, quiet, clean, and totally devoid of structure or humans. Three iguanas scampered for cover as the boat came close to the pristine, bleached shore. With only three and one half feet of draft on his new boat, he was able to safely anchor in the sandy shallows. The weather was ideal, only the ever-present ocean breeze rippling the water. Bryce dropped double bow anchors, allowing the gentle surf to keep the stern swimming platform steady toward the shore.

That done, Bryce untied the seven ropes that secured the large tent and began unrolling it across the back deck. As it unfurled, Malandra tumbled out of the last roll inside the tent and sprawled onto the deck followed by a small cylinder that had provided ample oxygen inside the tightly rolled bundle. Groggy from the cocktail Bryce had given him at dawn, Malandra looked around at his surroundings, confusion writ large on his face as he struggled against the stainless steel cuffs binding his ankles and wrists.

"Hi, Tony. Glad to see you could make it."

"What the hell is this? Where are we? We had a deal!"

"Yes, Tony. We had a deal. We still have a deal. You bought your life, and you will keep your life." Bryce walked over to Malandra and pulled him up onto the upholstered bench seat along the starboard rail.

"What the hell is going on?" Malandra asked as Bryce clipped a half dozen fishing weights to his leg cuffs, then tethered the cuff chain to the railing with a second chain.

"If you don't do exactly as I say, or perhaps think you can escape while I'm asleep, these lead weights will convince you to behave, since they will take you to the bottom of this ocean as sure as hot air will rise. We'll sleep on board tonight, then go ashore in the morning." Bryce went below and came out with two plastic glasses and a bottle of wine. "Sauvignon blanc. Still chilled. I hope you enjoy it. Salute."

Bryce straightened the tent Malandra had been rolled up in and folded it until it was the size of a small bed. "That should be comfortable enough for you. Better than you deserve, at any rate," he said as he poured another round and handed Malandra a plastic bag full of sharp cheddar and crackers, then opened one for himself. They ate in silence, then Bryce tossed Malandra a blanket and disappeared into the hold for a good night's sleep in the plush captain's suite.

Morning dawned clear and blue, not a cloud to be seen in the unpolluted sky. Bryce bounded up the stairwell and threw Malandra a granola bar and a bottle of water, then began pumping air into a little rubber dinghy. By mid-morning, he had it inflated and loaded with supplies. He rowed ashore and piled the gear and tools on the sand well above the high-water line, then repeated the process into the early afternoon until he had everything ashore.

"Now it's your turn, Tony. I'll unlock this leg and help you down the ladder, but the other leg will still have the lead weights on, so I would advise you to cooperate. Gravity is a harsh task master."

Bryce tied the dinghy tight to the gunwale and steadied the bobbing as Malandra navigated the ladder, dragging five pounds of lead and stainless steel behind his left leg. On shore, Bryce removed the weights and allowed Malandra to walk up the beach to stretch and relieve himself while he dragged the little boat above the high-tide ripples in the sand. He secured it with ropes tied to two sand stakes, a precaution against a sudden wind, then ordered Malandra to sit by a small tree. He chained his hobble to the tree with twenty feet of slack to allow movement. "Sorry, Tony, but something deep inside me says not to trust you roaming free." He set up a one-man tent next to the little tree and threw Malandra a pillow and two blankets. "Make yourself at home, Tony, I have work to do."

"What the hell are we doing, Bryce? You promised to let me go free if I gave you the money."

"All in good time, my friend. All in good time."

Satisfied that Malandra was no threat at his six, Bryce began erecting the large outfitter's tent with the zippered door and canvas floor. The tent was bulky, and this was typically a two-man job, but there was no way he could let Malandra handle a tent pole or hammer. He was happy to struggle alone. Once propped up and staked out, he carefully laid out a large tarp in front of it and then unfolded a large mat to wipe their feet on, hoping to leave dirt, dust, and sand outside. Next, he unfolded the medium tent inside the large one after carefully dusting it, then unrolled a second mat just in front of it. Now, there was little chance for sand or dirt to infiltrate the inner sanctum and little opportunity for insects to do so. He exited and painstakingly dusted off his cargo bags, carrying his equipment inside the double structure.

The sky was layering pinks over lavender above the settling sun as Bryce finished setting up camp. After he ran the fifty-foot electric cord through the corners of the tent doors, he connected it to the small gas generator. He carried two floor lamps and a small HEPA air-filtration unit into the inner tent, plugged them into the extension cord, and turned on the generator.

Bryce walked into the water and swam to the boat, weighed anchor, and moved it into deeper water in case of a squall, then triple anchored it. *You can never be too safe, especially in the wilderness.* He dropped the third anchor, secured the lines, and swam to shore.

"Now what?" Malandra asked, more nervous by the minute, confused as he watched the progression of the day.

"Oh, we'll work things out as we progress. You'll see. It will all be perfectly laid out and legal. Don't worry, Tony. Trust me," he added as he set up two beach chairs and opened a cooler. "Beer?"

"Cold beer would be pretty awesome right now, Bryce," Tony said, his eyes flitting about, unsure.

Bryce popped the top and handed him a two-dollar can of Corona, no glass to use as a weapon. He saved the hundred-dollar Châteauneuf-du-Pape for himself. "Cheers! A toast to our newfound freedom. Vive la liberte!" he bellowed, loud enough for the iguanas on the other side of the island to hear. He threw Malandra a bag of beef jerky and cheese and opened a bag for himself after setting a pot of water on the little backpacking stove to boil. "Bon appétit!"

Not having eaten since the granola bars in the morning, they enjoyed their quiet repast for several minutes. Bryce tossed him a second beer, poured himself another glass of wine, then poured the boiling water and mixed two pouches of Mountain House Turkey Tetrazzini. They ate quietly to the accompaniment of the surf washing the sand clean. The sun settled, painting a deep mauve behind the watery horizon as Bryce enjoyed his third glass of wine. He stood and finished his glass, then set it inside the cooler. "One more?" he asked as he held aloft another beer.

"Sure."

"OK. Then crawl into your tent and get some sleep. The bed on the boat would be more comfortable, but it's such a beautiful night, I'll sleep ashore to make sure you don't get into any mischief." He reclined in the lawn chair, stared up at the stars, and was asleep in minutes.

41

GOLDEN-PINK SUN WAS GLIMMERING OVER BLUE-BLACK OCEAN when Bryce awoke, stretched, and surveyed his domain. He fired up his little stove and put water on to boil, then ran to the water and dove in. He swam briefly, cleansing himself in the pristine water, then walked up the beach and roused Malandra. "Let's get you cleaned up for the day, prisoner number one," he said as he unlocked the long chain from the hobble and helped him to his feet. He led Malandra to the water and walked him in until the water reached his chest. "Clean up," he said as he handed Malandra a tube of biodegradable soap. A few minutes later, he led Malandra back to the camp and sat him in the beach chair while he made two mugs of coffee and opened a bag of donuts. They ate in silence, Malandra's eyes darting constantly, involuntarily, at Bryce.

"Time to get down to business," Bryce said as he picked up a small dowel wrapped with cloth at one end. He unrolled it and let the inshore breeze unfurl the small flag against the brightening sun as he planted it in the sand.

Justice Cay was written in red ink.

"What the hell is that supposed to mean?" Malandra asked as he watched the flag ripple in the breeze.

"This is your special island, bought and paid for by the wages of your labor, Tony." He pointed toward the name on the back of the boat, Justice Cay, now illuminated in the bright morning sun.

"So, what are you gonna do, just leave me cuffed and stranded on this little sandbox?"

"Be patient. It will all make sense as we progress," Bryce said as he opened a neatly folded piece of paper. He walked to the small flag wafting in the breeze, took a sip of his coffee, and began to read out loud.

"WHEN, in the course of human Events, it becomes necessary for one People to dissolve the Political Bands which have connected them to another, and to assume among the Powers of the Earth, the separate and equal Station to which the Laws of Nature and of Nature's God entitle them, a decent Respect to the Opinions of Mankind requires that they should declare the causes which impel them to the Separation."

"What are you spewing about now? Jesus, Thompson, have you lost it, or what?"

"Patience, my friend. Patience!" Bryce took another sip of his coffee and continued.

"WE hold these Truths to be self-evident, that all Men are created equal, that they are endowed by their Creator with certain unalienable Rights, that among these are Life, Liberty, and the Pursuit of Happiness—That to secure these Rights, Governments are instituted among Men, deriving their just Powers from the Consent of the Governed, that whenever any Form of Government becomes destructive of these Ends, it is the Right of the People to alter or abolish it, and to institute new Government, laying its Foundation on such Principles, and organizing its Powers in such Form, as to them shall seem most likely to effect their Safety and Happiness."

"You've turned into a total whack job, Thompson."

"But when a long Train of Abuses and Usurpations interferes with the common good, it is the Right, it is the Duty, of the People to throw off such Government, and to provide new Guards for their future Security. Such has been the patient Sufferance of this populace; and such is now the Necessity which constrains them to alter their former Systems of Government."

"You're over the edge, Thompson."

"Since our former Government has failed to protect the innocent in favor of assuring the Rights of the Guilty, and they have been deaf to the Voice of Justice and of Consanguinity, we must therefore acquiesce in the Necessity of our Separation.

"We, therefore, the Representatives of Justice Cay, in General Congress, Assembled, appealing to the Supreme Judge of the World for the Rectitude of our Intentions, do, in the Name of the Free and Law-Abiding People of this Island, solemnly Publish and Declare, That we are, and of Right ought to be, a Free and Independent State. And for the support of this Declaration, we mutually pledge our Lives, our Fortunes, and our sacred Honor."

Bryce took his pen and signed the Declaration with a flourish.

"I refuse to sign. Therefore, you do not have a majority, and you've wasted a lot of time and effort," Malandra said with a forced laugh.

"You must have missed the part where it said the "free and law-abiding people of this island." You are neither free nor law-abiding. You are currently under arrest for murder and cannot make it to the polls, so the record shall show that this Declaration of Independence has passed with a unanimous vote."

"You can't just make a country."

"Why not?"

"What gives you the right?"

"The same right that gave the Spanish, the English, and the French the right to land on these many shores, plant a flag and declare ownership. The same right that gave Cortés free reign to murder and enslave thousands of free people and steal their gold and silver. The same right that allowed Pizarro to murder Atahualpa and plunder the wealth of the Incas in Peru. The same right that gave the northern Europeans dominion over the Native Americans, forcing them off the land they had owned for centuries."

"What right was that, if I may be so presumptuous to ask?"

"They had the most powerful weapons."

"That gives them the right? Can't we be a little more serious, Bryce?"

"Throughout the history of mankind, might has always dictated right. The history of mankind is the history of war, and that history has always been written by the victors. Furthermore, the European conquerors believed their actions were legal because they had a charter from their king authorizing their actions. It was all legal because it was written down.

"In fact, it was precisely this same right that you assumed for yourself when you took the lives of multiple people for the profit and the challenge of your game. The same right you assumed for yourself when you killed my brother, my wife, and my only child."

"That was different, and I have not only explained and apologized, I have paid you for it. Twenty million in return for my life. That was the deal. I would bring them back in an instant if I could. He was coming after me, and I did what any animal would do. I protected myself. You know as well as anyone that this is a mean, cruel world, and it is kill or be killed. Eat or be eaten. It's the law of the jungle. That is really the only law that matters in this world. If one animal wants to eat, another plant or animal is forfeit. I wanted to live worse than the others. I had a stronger survival instinct. The strong survive. The weak perish. That's the way it's always been. Darwin was right," Malandra concluded.

"Point made, but in the jungle, the rules are the same across the board. You were playing by different rules than everyone else. In an advanced society, people live by an agreed upon higher standard of rules. By setting your own rules, you had an unfair advantage, like playing cards with a marked deck. That's called cheating, Tony."

"No, that's called smart. In this world, we are born, we live briefly, and then we suffer and die and are forgotten, except for the handful of people who make it into the history books. Most peoples' lives are a blip of meaningless struggle."

"I've always believed that there should be a line in the sand that we shouldn't cross. Particularly doctors. I will give plenty of morphine or fentanyl to someone in pain, especially if they are near death, but I won't intentionally overdose them. I will not willingly kill them. To me, that crosses the line. Once you cross that line, it's easier to continue, to blur the edges of who deserves to live and who deserves to die. That appears to be exactly what your trajectory has been."

"We all have to die. It's just the timing that's different."

"Then you shouldn't mind if I alter your timing."

"Except that we had a verbal contract, and you are a man of your word."

"Yes, I am," Bryce answered as he poured them each a fresh cup of coffee. "Now, I have drawn up a constitution for our new country. Mr. Madison and the Founding Fathers did such a good job, I modeled it after theirs." He handed a copy to Malandra. "You will notice that it is much shorter. Since our population is so small, we have no need for two houses of government, and the Supreme Court will have but one member. You will also note that I have adhered to my original campaign promise such that there is no authorization for the death penalty.

"I now move to ratify this constitution as written. I call the vote. All in favor shall signify by saying Aye! All opposed shall signify by saying Nay! What say you, Thompson?

"Aye!

"Let the Record show that it has passed by unanimous, roll call vote. I nominate Bryce Thompson as president, speaker of the house, and chief justice. I call the vote. All in favor say Aye!

"Aye!

"Unanimous again."

"What kind of mockery of government is this? You don't have the power to enforce any laws you arbitrarily make," Malandra said.

"Of course, I do. I have the consent of the free and law-abiding citizens as well as complete power over the populace of this country, as much or more than any other government that imposes their will on the governed. I have that power until someone more powerful, with more soldiers or bigger guns, forces me out. That's another law of the jungle that you, of all people, should understand. If you think you can stop me, be my guest. As to making a mockery of government, that's what you've been doing for years. You have taken the powers and prerogatives of government and used them to your private benefit, at the expense of others. That is exactly why people have formed governments for centuries—to protect themselves from enemies, foreign and domestic."

"It would be total anarchy if everyone formed their own government when it suited their whim," Malandra countered.

"There have been times of anarchy throughout history. There's always an element of anarchy when a government is not strong enough to control the populace. Who made the rules in Russia on the first of January in 1917? The czar. Who made the rules in Russia on the first of January in 1923? The Communist Party. Who was right and who was wrong? In between, there was total anarchy. Civil war. Carnage. Deaths in the millions. Atrocities by those with the most guns. On both sides. Look at Somalia or even Mexico today. Large areas of those countries are lawless, controlled by gangs because the central government is too weak to control those gangs. Who is right and who is wrong?"

Bryce took a deep breath and went on. "In the final analysis, there are tens of thousands of laws on the books, but they can help some people and hurt others, particularly when taken out of context. How about the laws in America in 1860 that said all citizens were equal, while all the laws supported ownership of slaves and protected the rights of white male citizens? The right to flog a slave who disobeyed? The right to castrate or hang a black man who looked at a white woman? The right to beat his wife? Who was right and who was wrong? Were things that much better a hundred years later? In 1960, civil rights workers had to march in the streets, be shot and stabbed, beaten and hung, until the Civil Rights Act of 1964 was finally passed. Even then, it took years for things to normalize. Who was right and who was wrong?

"Everyone in power claims they are right. It is only with the power of education and the retrospectoscope that light is shed on darker times. In the final analysis, despite the thousands of laws that have been passed over the millennia, there is only one law that consistently holds."

"And what, pray tell, is that?"

"Do unto others as you would have them do unto you."

"Oh! Great. Now you're going to throw superstitious Bible quotes at me. Who says that is right or wrong?"

"Because it covers everything equally. If it's good for you, it should be equally good for others. If it's bad for you, if you don't want it done to you, then you shouldn't do it to others. It is a universal rule of fairness, and if everyone followed it, there would be peace. Unfortunately, humans are animals and mostly fend for their own benefit. Let's face it. Despite most people professing they believe in a deity, their actions do not mirror their words. In living their daily lives, most people are functional atheists."

Bryce took a sip and continued. "Look at how the European missionaries treated the 'savages' of Africa and South America. It was horrendous, with enslavement, persecution, flogging, even burning at the stake. For their own good, the good of their souls, of course. I ask you, who were the savage ones? And, during the Inquisition, how many people suffered at the hands of the clergy? And they got away with it, not because they were right but because they had the might. They were the majority, and they made the rules. It was sanctioned by the government and written down; therefore it was legal. In truth, it was all one big lie!"

"Oh, Bryce," Malandra scoffed. "You haven't kept up on your developmental psychology, have you? Don't you realize that the lie is an advanced developmental trait? It takes an advanced mind to weave a story that helps secure a future outcome. Most animals graze for food on a daily basis. Only a few plan ahead and store food for future use, but man not only plans for years in advance, he routinely uses deceit to outwit a competitor. And it wouldn't be possible without language, man's very own unique tool. Survival often depends on deceit. Every good general in every war uses misinformation to gain an advantage. Everyone lies. The development and use of language, for truth or for lying, for advancing our aims, is what makes us human."

"You say that as if it is a justification," Bryce countered.

"It's how the world works. The law of the jungle is very clear. Eat or be eaten. That is the way nature has evolved. The strong survive to pass on the better genes; the weak perish."

"No right? No wrong? Only win or lose? Is that all there is to this circus?"

"Afraid so, Bryce. We're just chance creatures of evolutionary development on this revolving rock. We just happen to be the most evolved of all the species, but in reality, we have no more meaning to our survival than that ant," he added as he pointed to an ant crawling across the sand. Malandra stomped his foot on the ant, crushing it instantly. "See what I mean? One minute we are alive, the next we are dead. Just one of billions of unimportant ants. We think we are important, the apex of the evolutionary chain, but I'll bet *Tyrannosaurus Rex* thought so too. No, we are but tiny, transient specks on a tiny speck of this solar system, which is a tiny speck of this galaxy, which is a tiny speck of the entire universe. And we'll be extinct too, someday. If there is a god who created this, he has one hell of a sense of humor. Now you want to hold me to an ancient law people claim was handed down by this sadistic god."

"That law historically has nothing to do with religion. I am as wary of religious types as anyone. When Socrates questioned the authority of the rulers in Greece and asked questions about their gods, they killed him. When Jesus of Nazareth questioned the authority of the Sadducees, they killed him. When the Catholics were in power, they killed the Protestants. When the Protestants were in power, they killed the Catholics. When the Muslims were in power, they killed the Hindus. And everyone killed the Jews.

"No, that law is not based on religion. It is founded on universal fairness. It was suggested by Confucius five centuries before Jesus of Nazareth quoted it. You don't need to posit a deity to be moral. Morality is the ideal to do what is more right than more wrong. More good than more bad. More fair than more unfair."

"And who is to define good?" Tony asked. "If there is no deity, there is no capital G Good, just constant interpretation and reinterpretation by lowly humans. We are born, we live, we die. And most humans live miserably. That's all there is."

. "Well said, Mr. Hobbes. But good and evil are usually self-evident."

"Untrue. They are relative, like everything else."

"No. What you really mean is that legal is relative, like the slave laws that were legal. If I took a pair of pliers and crushed each of your fingers for the sole purpose of watching you suffer, would that be relative? If we can't define good versus evil, if we can't discern a good act from an evil act, then what is the use of language other than a tool to manipulate, to obfuscate?"

"My point exactly. The smart survive; the weak perish."

"Based on your interpretation of right and wrong, you won't take umbrage at the next step in the development of this new country. Take off your sandals and wipe your feet completely on this mat. Then take this towel and wipe them again. Be sure to get the sand out from between your toes. I do not want a dirty interior," he added as he took off his sandals and cleaned his own feet, then unzipped the outer door and led Malandra inside. He zipped that door shut, then unzipped the inner tent and told Malandra to take the chair set up in the corner.

Malandra's eyes scanned the two chairs and the cot, the bright overhead lamps, and the air-purifier in the corner. But when he spied the impeccably clean folding table filled with medical machines and bundles carefully wrapped in sterile, surgical packaging, he lunged at Bryce and tried to throw his handcuffed arms around his neck. Bryce fell back against the tent wall as he instinctively thrust a hand up under the cuffs. Malandra tightened the little chain of the cuffs as tight as he could, but Bryce's large frame was too much for the smaller man. Bryce bent over rapidly, flipping Malandra over his back and hurtling him against the table. Bryce took two steps and smashed Malandra in the jaw, stunning him momentarily. He propped him into the chair and tied his waist to the chair with a piece of rope.

"What the hell is this?" Malandra asked, eyeing the surgical setup.

"Every citizen deserves his day in court. This is your hearing." He waited for Malandra to settle down, then stood and began. "This lawfully assembled court of Justice Cay is duly sworn and assembled. Antonio Malandra! You have been charged with the murder of thirteen people." He read the names slowly.

"Harold Swenson.
"Alexander Bancroft.
"Charles Corsello.
"Sean Peterson.
"Thomas Carter.
"Neil Jensen.
"Roman Emerson.

"William Zebrowski.

"Jill Downing.

"Detective Steven Willett.

"Detective William Thompson.

"Nicole Marie Thompson.

"Baby George William Thompson.

"How plead you?"

"Not guilty!" He spat the words at Bryce.

"This court has written and sworn testimony that you admitted forty-eight hours ago to killing these people." Bryce picked up the piece of paper. "I enter this as exhibit number one." He passed a copy to Malandra.

"Objection!" Malandra roared, so loud that six iguanas scampered for cover.

"Overruled," Bryce answered, his voice firm and controlled. "This court has written and sworn testimony that a member of this court personally examined the interior of your safe in New York. Inside, he found hundreds of thousands of dollars in cash, gold coins, and bullion, along with the names of several of the aforementioned victims and the amount of money profited from each of those murders. Attached is a picture of the inside of this safe and a picture of the names of several of the victims. I enter this as exhibit number two."

Malandra was slack-jawed as he saw the picture of the inside of his safe. "How the … Objection! Illegal search and seizure!"

"Overruled."

Bryce picked up a third piece of paper. "This court has written and sworn testimony that a member of this court, with reasonable cause, entered and examined the interior of your home and, as shown in this picture, found a chemical laboratory and chemical exhaust hood used for the making of a poisonous aerosol that you admitted to using to kill one William Thompson, one Nicole Thompson, and one unborn baby Thompson. I enter this as exhibit number three."

"Objection! Illegal entry. Illegal search."

"Overruled. You have already admitted to this. The court accepts these exhibits, and the prosecution rests its case."

If contempt could be felt, it was palpable in Bryce's glare as he turned to Malandra and said, "The defense may now address the court. What say you?"

"What difference does it make? This is a rigged jury. You hold all the cards. You have the might."

"Are you saying that you have nothing to say to this court in your defense?"

"It's like I said before. It's the law of the jungle. Kill or be killed. Eat or be eaten. Survival of the fittest. You quote a Bible passage to me as the one rule of the land. I say the Bible has no authority here. It is an ancient, superstitious history book and has nothing to offer educated mankind. There is no god! If there is, he abandoned this rotating dirt clod to fend for itself billions of years ago. If there is a god, he also created a system where you have to kill to stay alive. An anteater has to kill ants to eat. Is that murder? A lioness pounces on the gazelle to feed her cubs. Is that murder? An elephant steps on a nest walking to the water hole. Is it guilty because it crushed six ducklings?"

Bryce nodded. "It's true we kill to eat, but you have offered no defense for killing one of the same species, which is the definition of murder. Pure evil does exist, and a serial killer is proof of that."

"Evil is relative. There is no such thing as pure evil."

"We don't have to go back beyond the last century to see pure evil. Adolph Hitler exterminated six million people because of their race and religion. Joseph Stalin caused the death of twenty million of his own people. Idi Amin butchered a half million of his countrymen to hold onto power. Pol Pot, two million. Oh, yes, pure evil does exist."

"Semantics!"

"You killed for no nobler cause than profit. Or was it pleasure? Most animals kill what they need to eat. Rats and weasels kill more than they can eat—kill for pleasure. That's the company you're in, Tony. Rats and weasels. Was it pleasurable, Tony? Was it fun, excelling at the challenge? Winning at the game? Was it an adrenaline rush?"

"They were all guilty. Guilty of dishonesty. Guilty of business fraud. Guilty of adultery. Guilty of emotional abuse. You name it … well, all except your brother and … what's her name."

Bryce felt the bile rise in his throat. He wanted to smash Malandra's face. Instead, he nearly whispered. "Her name was Nicole."

"Yeah. I just went blank for a minute trying to save my ass. But the others were guilty. Hell, we're all guilty. But since there is no god, there are no rules. You proved it yourself. You gave me several examples that proved there is no right or wrong, only more might versus less might, and the victors make the rules and write the history. But we had an agreement. I turned over twenty million dollars. In return, you promised not to kill me. So, where do we go from here?"

"That's it? That's the totality of your defense?"

"I played by the rules of the jungle. They could have done the same."

"Not true. They played by the agreed upon rules of a society. A society that allowed you to get a good education, avoid going to war, make a great living, and live in a nice home protected by employees of that very society. And protect you they did, most notably in Montana. But you decided to live by your own rules. You broke every covenant of a civilized society."

"This is nothing but a shit show, a kangaroo court, and all the citizens of this country know it. We have a deal, so I say flog me or torture me, and let's get this over with and get on with our lives."

"Then the defense rests?"

"Sure," he snarled, looking away.

"Then it is the unanimous judgment of this court, duly and legally sanctioned by the laws of this country, that defendant Antonio Malandra is found guilty of thirteen counts of murder in the first degree, and, whereas the constitution of this country does not authorize capital punishment, you are hereby sentenced to life imprisonment without the possibility of parole."

"So. You are going to chain me to this island until I starve to death, aren't you, Thompson? A hypocrite, just like every other lowly, miserable animal on this planet. You think you are so high and mighty with your sanctimonious words, but you're just another animal fighting for the upper hand. A charlatan in priest's clothing. You make me sick. At least I'm honest about who I am."

"Tony, you have pushed me into territory I never thought I would have to traverse. All my training and all my ethics plead for mercy. But I also know that if you go free, you will continue to hurt others, and that would weigh on my conscience with an unbearable heaviness, my very own Sisyphean rock. You have forced me onto this plank I must walk. I'm an angel if I let you go, but I'm a demon if I let you hurt others, and I have no reason to doubt that you would hurt others. Your word is without honor.

"Therefore, it is the decision of this court that the defendant was and remains a danger to society, and if allowed any form of parole, he would further endanger innocent lives. It is the responsibility of this court to ensure the safety of society. Furthermore, it is the judgment of this court that the punishment should fit the crime. Since the defendant deprived the deceased of their freedom forever, it is the determination of this court that the defendant shall have his freedom likewise deprived forever. And in his solitary imprisonment, he can ponder his crime and his punishment until such time as natural causes will remove him from this earth."

With that, Bryce picked up a syringe, walked behind the chair, and injected it into Malandra's trapezius muscle. He was asleep in minutes.

42

"WAKE UP, TONY! WAKE UP! I KNOW YOU CAN HEAR ME. YOU have slept for nearly sixty hours, but the monitors show you are rousing. Wake up so we can have a discussion, one-sided though it will be. I have you hooked up to a makeshift EEG machine, and I see the spikes of brain activity as I talk. The ECG readout shows a steady heart rhythm. Your pulse rose quickly from sixty to eighty-eight, so your body is responding normally to my voice today.

"Tony, you have imprisoned me in my own private purgatory for the last few months, and I have struggled to break free. You tell me that there is no god or heaven, but I am about to teach you that there is a hell.

"You gave me a little run for my money when you went into spinal shock after I transected your spinal cord between C1 and C2. I had to give you nearly four liters of fluid and a norepinephrine drip to keep your blood pressure up for a few hours, but you're relatively young and healthy and came through it nicely. Oh! Now I know you're awake. That little tidbit of information just made your pulse jump to 120. Perfect.

"After I sedated you, I placed a large-bore IV and started a propofol drip. Then I connected an insulated spinal needle to the Bovie machine, slipped the needle into the space between the vertebrae, and passed a coagulating current little by little until all your muscles went limp. It took a few hours to pull you out of spinal shock, but good doctoring kept you alive. Just as promised.

"This would be lost on a layman, but as a pathologist, you will understand the purity of what I have done. I slipped the needle upward and inward along the base of the skull with little twitches of current until the trapezius muscle began to twitch, then I obliterated the eleventh cranial nerve, the spinal accessory, on both sides. Now you can move nothing below the neck.

"I left the vagus nerve, the tenth cranial nerve, intact, for reasons that will soon be clear. I found the twelfth cranial nerve, the hypoglossal, from the front and coagulated that. Now, you cannot move your tongue. You will never tell anyone how you came to be in this condition. The fifth, the trigeminal, I accessed from inside your mouth, so you can't taste or move your cheek and jaw. Up on the mastoid bone, I located the stylomastoid foramen and cauterized the seventh cranial nerve, and now your muscles of facial expression no longer respond to your brain's commands.

"The eyes were easy, Tony. I hit the abducens, the trochlear, and the oculomotor nerves, so you can't communicate with eye movements. It was easy to hit the optic nerves, so although the sun is bright and beautiful today, everything is probably very dark in there, unless I missed some fibers, and you see splotches of gray here and there. But, even if you could, you can't open your eyelids to enjoy another sunrise.

"Lastly, when I am finished explaining everything, I will destroy your bones of hearing, and to prevent post-op infection, I have some concentrated gentamicin solution which will kill almost any bacteria in the middle ear compartment. You remember your pharmacology, don't you, Tony? You remember how ototoxic gentamicin is, even diluted? So, even if destroying the bones of hearing doesn't work completely, the gentamicin will erode the eighth cranial nerve. You will never again hear another bird sing to the sunrise. You will never see another golden sunset. Or hear another Beethoven symphony.

"You will never hear a thirteen-year-old girl squeal with delight at the sight of a new dress instead of crying in despair as she is being molested by a sick son of a bitch who claims he is doing her a favor.

"This is how I will leave you, Tony. The only sense you have left is your sense of smell, which I didn't know how to get rid of, but it's just as well, because you will be able to smell yourself as you lie in your own excrement.

"Additionally, you still have feeling on the top of your scalp, and I will visit you once a year in the nursing home and give you a little electric shock on top of your head just so you don't forget me. Each time I visit, and you feel this twelve-volt zing, that will be your signal for you to remember my wife and my unborn baby lying on the floor, helpless and gasping for their last breath.

"You see, Tony, I am keeping my word. I am letting you live. I don't want you dead. Killing you would be merciful. That would be doing you a favor. Death is no punishment. Death is peaceful. No, no! I want you to have a long life. A long life with your brain floating isolated inside your perfectly healthy body, the feeding tube in your jejunum keeping the nutrients flowing for years so you can lie there and think about how smart you are and how stupid I am.

"I have a private room reserved in the best nursing home in Nassau, and the administrator is very, very motivated to make sure you get the best of care. You see, I explained to him that you are my brother and I have faith that you will recover from your stroke, so he gets to keep this boat for his own use, and if he keeps you alive for ten years, he gets the title. Additionally, once a year, he and your doctor will each receive an envelope containing ten thousand dollars in cash as further motivation to make sure my brother gets the best of the best. All paid for with your money.

"I am sending the bulk of the cash from your safe to Montana, where it will be delivered to Detective Willett's family. Between that and his life insurance money, they won't be destitute.

"Lastly, I transferred three million into an account for Jill's parents, the rightful beneficiaries of her life insurance, and they can at least live in comfort in their retirement.

"With what's left of your blood money, I plan to do something I have always thought would be fulfilling. You told me once that I couldn't save them all. Of course, you were right. But I can save a few, so I plan to go to Africa and use your money to build a hospital in a little isolated village Nicole and I visited on our trekking safari and try to make life a little better for one small corner of the world. I'll drill a well and build a water filtration system along with a sewage system. We will build wooden houses with floors instead of mud huts. There will be plenty left to build a new school and hire a teacher.

"And it's all perfectly legal and sanctioned by the duly appointed court of this country. And how do we know its legal, Tony? Because it's all written down.

"But don't worry, I won't neglect you. I'll fly back once a year to check on you and make sure you're getting the best of everything. Then my promise will be honored. You will live, Tony. Hopefully, you will live a long, long life. You will have no responsibilities, no schedule, no stress. Just lie there and think. Because that is all you will be able to do, your brain isolated from the outside world, a tiny island floating inside your cerebrospinal fluid, perfectly intact.

"If there is a heaven, I know my family is there now. But you are about to find out that there truly is a hell. You can lie there and think about how you were beaten, what you could have done differently, what you did wrong, and the inescapability of your sentence. You can think about what is right and what is wrong, what is good and what is evil. You didn't believe in hell before, but after ten or twenty or thirty years, you will understand that hell does exist, and you have just entered the portals."

EPILOGUE

A NEW DAY IN A NEW YEAR SHOULD BE GREETED BY A NEW SUN, and the astonishing golden globe, unfiltered through the rain-freshened air, did not disappoint. Bryce stood on the tiny porch of his cabin looking out at the village, sipping his African *kahawa*, coffee he had grown and nourished and ground and brewed with his own hands. He looked across the village and saw a low, muddy spot by the well that needed filling and made a mental note. The village children no longer had to make the three-mile trek for water every day. When he arrived ten years prior, the villagers were living in mud huts. Now, wooden structures graced the area on raised foundations with snake-resistant thresholds, stoves instead of floor pits, metal chimneys instead of dried-mud vent holes, sewage lines instead of random waste, and screens to keep out malaria-carrying mosquitoes.

HOSPITALI NICOLE was full of patients, and people were coming for miles to see *Daktari Thompson*. Today he would start training a new class of fifteen-year-olds how to draw blood and prepare slides, and the sixteen-year-olds would graduate to looking at those slides for the telltale signs of disease, especially malaria, malaria that had dropped ninety percent since his arrival. The teens had already mastered most of the basic skills of nursing starting at age twelve, and the interested ones began learning to diagnose disease, suture wounds, and assist him in surgery at eighteen. The gifted ones became his physician assistants by twenty-two.

On his birthday, the village elders had presented him with a mother-of-pearl necklace on which was carved *"Familia Yangu."* They explained with pride that Bryce had been formally adopted, and this meant that the entire village was now "My Family."

Bryce no longer returned to America, the thirst to see Malandra punished long since quenched. Tim and Monica Downing traveled to Tanzania nearly every year to visit. Family was the word they used as well.

Bryce finished his coffee as he looked around his modest yard. The tomatoes in the raised garden plots were showing a hint of red peeking out from under the green. He watered them gently and pulled a single weed before walking to the hospital. He knew Nicole would have approved.

The End